THE MAGIC TOUCH

Lady Hope is residing with her Aunt Constance whilst her parents tour Europe. At a dinner party, she finds herself drawn to the captivating Beaumont: philanthropist and magic lanternist. Intrigued by the idea of his shows at the local fair, but unable to attend as a lone gentle-woman, Hope hits upon a solution — adopting a male disguise, she attends Beaumont's performances incognito. As the two grow ever closer, will there be a magical time ahead for them?

PATRICIA KEYSON

THE MAGIC TOUCH

Complete and Unabridged

LINFORD
Leicester

First published in Great Britain in 2013

First Linford Edition
published 2016

A catalogue record for this book is available
from the British Library.

ISBN 978–1–4448–2945–7

Published by
F. A. Thorpe (Publishing)
Anstey, Leicestershire

Set by Words & Graphics Ltd.
Anstey, Leicestershire
Printed and bound in Great Britain by
T. J. International Ltd., Padstow, Cornwall

This book is printed on acid-free paper

1

Hope was restless. She stretched and tried not to think about being out in the freedom of the garden at home. Fortunately, her Aunt Constance was paying her no attention, as she was perusing the menus the cook had sent up from the kitchen. Hope looked out of the window and wondered how she was going to endure her time here in London if she had to remain cooped up indoors for most of her stay whilst her aunt was still in mourning for her husband. There were so many things Hope would like to see and do. Everything was much larger and louder than she was used to in the small town where her home was. She certainly didn't begrudge her parents a trip to the continent, but she missed them a great deal. She also missed the independence they afforded her. Hope's wish had been to be included in their tour abroad, but no invitation had been forthcoming. On the point of inviting herself, she witnessed an intimate look pass between her parents, and immediately understood that this was a two-person trip.

'Hope, are you listening to me?'

She hadn't been, and when she glanced at Aunt Constance, she wished she had paid attention. Her aunt was an intimidating woman, and now she looked positively ferocious.

'Sorry, Aunt. I was thinking about my mother and father.'

It was a true, if selective, reply.

'I understand.' Her aunt's face softened a little. 'Of course you miss them. I am arranging a dinner party to cheer you up. Would you like to inspect the menus and guest list?'

Hope smiled her assent. It would be fun to make new acquaintances, even friends. At nearly twenty-six, she was old enough to take care of herself. In practice, though, this had not been borne out, as she was on her way to ending up a spinster living with her parents. Since the horrible day when she'd overheard an erstwhile admirer telling a friend he thought he could do better than the plain Hope Richmond, she had distanced herself from invitations. It had taken Hope a long time to build up her self-confidence following that. She hadn't dared confide in her parents, as her father might have taken his fists to the man. But now she was able to face her reflection in the mirror with renewed self-assurance. Perhaps while she was in London she could strive to acquire increased poise. It was something to consider.

'Who are these people you've invited, Aunt?'

Constance continued, 'You will see I have included a few gentlemen who may be suitable escorts for you.'

Hope now realised the dinner was an excuse to present her with any male who might make a good husband, or indeed any kind of husband at all. A few years ago she would have jumped at the chance, but lately she had found other things to occupy her mind. She had a wide range of pastimes, including literature, painting, and — recently — anything remotely connected to her parents' travels. She envied her father rooting about in the historical remains of Ancient Rome, and her mother being transported by the exquisite art galleries. She envisaged the heat, the scents of exotic flowers and the foreign speech. It could prove a distraction to imagine what the local people were saying. Or, better still, a spur to learn their language and take them by surprise one day by conversing in their native tongue. Returning her attention to the pieces of paper, she listened distractedly to her aunt's exposition.

'. . . and then there's James Henderson. He's a good-looking and respectable young man.'

By omission, Aunt Constance had painted a dismal picture of her guest, and Hope lost interest right away. If he was not exciting, resourceful, and could not amuse her, she wouldn't be interested in him. Her vivid imagination had filled her head with romance and a sense of adventure; she would not trade them for anything less. Careful not to shatter her aunt's good intentions on her behalf, Hope deflected the remarks about the gentleman in question and said, 'All this food. Goodness me, I shall have to let the seams of my dresses out.'

Constance gave a snort which was as much as Hope had heard in the way of laughter coming from her. Then she said, 'I'm sure your mother taught you to eat only small amounts of each course, or even to miss one or two. There are eight, after all.'

Hope scrutinized the menu. She felt it was quite unfair that they would be eating vast amounts. She'd seen children on the streets begging for food, despite the Poor Law having been in existence for over fifty years. However, she dared not speak of this to her aunt.

'It will be very good, I'm sure.'

'You will be more aware of the gentleman sitting at your side than the food, my dear. That's exactly as it should be. Now, it's well on time you went up to change.'

'What's wrong with me?' Hope looked down at her ensemble, which she had thought to be ideal for a day at home with her aunt.

'It's nearly time for luncheon. I have invited Lady Padstock and her two daughters to join us. I believe you met them last year when you were staying in London.'

Indeed she had. Their impeccable dress sense, manners and decorum had dazzled her. They were also beautiful.

Then Hope remembered that she'd have to change several times a day whilst she was staying here. It wasn't something she was used to, but it might be amusing. At home, her mother hadn't given a hoot what she wore. One time, she'd taken the liberty of staying in her nightwear all day, and neither of her parents had appeared to notice. Her mother, when engrossed in her painting, would sometimes forget to eat or to get the cook to prepare some sort of collation for them. Going upstairs to her room, she thought of home; it was often filled with laughter, occasionally with silence, but always replete with love.

When she got to her room, Hope was surprised to find the maid she'd been assigned there.

'Hello, Edna. What are you doing here?' When she uttered the words, she knew she'd said the wrong thing as she watched the young girl's cheeks become even rosier. Quickly, she said, 'Oh, how foolish I am. You're here to help me change. Which outfit shall we choose? I'm afraid I haven't many and I'm sure they've been paraded already.'

Edna bobbed her head. 'The green and pink one is lovely, Lady Hope.'

Hope fingered the fine material. It had been her mother's. She lifted it to her nose and inhaled. It still vaguely possessed her mother's familiar scent.

'A good choice, Edna. Thank you.'

After the dress had been arranged and tweaked, Hope said, 'Edna, what do you know of a gentleman named James Henderson? He's on the guest list for the dinner my aunt is arranging. I know nothing of these people, and suppose I should find out a little of their background.' Hope knew she was being naughty, as she could always ask her aunt these questions, but she had the feeling Edna would be more forthright with her.

She watched as Edna screwed up her pert little nose. 'I suppose I should say he's . . . ' The silence intrigued Hope, and she waited for Edna to continue without making it look as if she were hurrying the girl. ' . . . a passionate young man. In all honesty, I don't think I can, though.' When Hope burst into giggles, Edna joined in, and the two clutched each other to prevent themselves from falling over.

'Begging your pardon, my lady,'

gasped Edna, righting herself and holding her stomach. 'Now, if Mr Beaumont is on that list, that's a different kettle of fish.' Hope felt she couldn't embarrass Edna by asking more, at least not today, but the name embedded itself in her subconscious. 'I think I should see to your hair now, Lady Hope.'

'Oh, but you spent such a long time on it this morning, I really don't think it necessary.' Then she thought of Mary and Isabella Padstock. Perhaps Edna could tame her tresses into something grand and pleasing to the eye. But if truth be told, she couldn't bear any more time in front of the mirror today.

'It's up to you, my lady, but . . . ' Edna reached out and twisted some wispy strands of hair which had escaped from Hope's braids. 'I don't know how it manages to come down; I pinned it well. Maybe it's because it's so fine.'

'Or maybe it's because I don't keep my head still and bound about too much. Aunt Constance rebuked me when I ran down the stairs this morning. Apparently it's not how I should behave. It's quite different at home; Mother shrieks with laughter when we have races down the banisters.'

'Your mother sounds very . . .'

'I believe 'different' is the word you're looking for. Certainly Father's family thought so at first. But people can't help loving her. Even Aunt Constance doesn't disapprove of her quite as much as she used to. But you don't want to hear all this.' Hope smiled at the maid. 'If you have to see to my hair again, shall we get on with it?'

As Edna removed the pins from her sable-coloured hair and brushed it, Hope studied her own features in the mirror. Her face was strong and well-defined, her complexion unblemished. Sparkling eyes twinkled back at her and it seemed a playful smile was never far away. Yet, despite all that, she would not describe herself as pretty, unlike the Padstock girls with their porcelain skin and blonde curls.

Edna smiled at her in the mirror. 'If you don't mind me saying, you have beautiful eyes. They're such a clear, bright green.' She tucked another pin in place.

'Thank you, Edna. I don't regard myself as a vain person, but I'm always happy to receive compliments.'

'There, all done. I expect Her Grace is waiting for you to join her so that you will be ready to receive your guests together. I heard that Lady Mary Padstock is engaged to be married, and I imagine you will hear all the details of the wedding arrangements. It's going to be a grand occasion.'

A wedding was something to look forward to, although there was no reason why she would be invited. There must be other things happening here as well. She grabbed Edna's hand. 'We must make the most of my stay in London. There is so much to see and do. Please say you'll help me escape from my aunt's company, at least for some of the time. I love her dearly, but I long to be with people nearer my own age.'

Edna looked worried. 'I'll do my best, as long as you don't get me into so much trouble that I lose my position.'

Hope thought fondly of her own maid, Ruth. She had wanted her to come to London, but just as they were about to set off, news had come that Ruth's mother and father had been struck down with influenza. Ruth had been allowed to go home to care for them and her younger siblings. It had been a wrench to bid farewell to her parents *and* her trusted maid, but Hope would write letters and try to cheer Ruth up. After the sickness was over, her maid would be able to enjoy some free time with her family.

At the top of the stairs Hope was tempted to slide down the banister, but instead decorously made her way to talk to her aunt until Stevenson, the butler, announced the arrival of their guests.

Hope's mind wandered as the others talked and laughed through the meal. Her attention was caught by the mention of Mr Beaumont.

'A very strange person,' announced Lady Padstock. 'He may be rich, but Isabella knows I regard him as an inappropriate match for her.'

'Oh, Mama, as if I'd even consider him. No, The Honourable James Henderson would suit me very well.'

Hope glanced at her aunt and wasn't surprised to see her face was like thunder. She was startled to find a small butterfly of excitement spreading its wings in her stomach. Luncheon now seemed appetising in more ways than one.

She toyed with her knife and fork before addressing the young woman opposite her. 'Your hair's so pretty, Isabella. It becomes you well. I'm sure you must have the pick of every gentleman in London. Do you wish to follow Mary to the altar shortly?'

'My hair is looked after meticulously,

Hope. Good grooming is a lesson you would do well to learn. My guess is that your maid isn't doing her best. Or perhaps your hair was neglected shamefully before you arrived here. If you wish, I could send someone to advise you.'

Perhaps she ought to take Isabella up on her kind proposal. She smiled at her. 'Thank you; I appreciate your offer. But don't let's talk of me. Tell me something of James Henderson.' Without looking in her aunt's direction, Hope knew she was eavesdropping. 'If you hold him in high regard, then I'm sure he would prove good company.' Perhaps she should not have cast aside James Henderson so quickly if someone as agreeable as Isabella had him in her sights.

Isabella fidgeted, and Hope guessed she was debating how much to give away about her intended victim. Eventually, the reply came. 'If James Henderson attends a mutual function, I shall be pleased to introduce you.'

'That's most kind.' Mindful of her aunt's advice to eat small portions, Hope put her knife and fork down. 'And Mr Beaumont? Is there any particular reason why he doesn't fit your requirements?' Hope wanted to find out all she could about the guests at the dinner her aunt was arranging.

Aunt Constance raised her voice. 'Mary, tell us about your forthcoming wedding. It's a very exciting time for you and your family.'

Mary's eyes lit up as she nodded her head. 'Everyone except Father! He's appalled at the expense.'

Lady Padstock looked horrified. 'Mary! What a thing to say.'

The attention was on Mary now. Hope was pleased with the progress she'd made in her small talk, but disappointed that Isabella had revealed nothing about the mysterious Mr Beaumont. The subject of Mary's lavish nuptials occupied the rest of the luncheon conversation.

By the time their carriage arrived to

deliver the Padstock ladies to their home, Hope was ready to collapse in a heap.

'You behaved with decorum, Hope. I'm sure it couldn't have been easy for you,' said Aunt Constance. 'Those girls can be wearisome. But you could learn a lot from them.' Her aunt glanced at Hope's hair. 'If you wish, I will send for Isabella's maid.'

Hope laughed. 'I'm not sure she would be successful, however experienced and talented she is. I'm perfectly happy with Edna. My hair is very fine and likes to spring free in order to embarrass me.' As she spoke, Hope fingered her hair, enjoying the silky texture of it despite its waywardness. Briefly, she thought of her mother's thick curls. What luxury to be able to let a glorious mane unfold around one's shoulders.

'Very well. Now, would you care to read to me? Or would you prefer to spend some time with your embroidery?'

Embroidery was something Hope was not good at. She had no interest in it and quickly tired of the fine stitches she had to make. After even a short session, the cloth resembled a crumpled napkin. 'I'd like to read to you. Shall we continue with the book we started yesterday, or do you have another preference?' So far, reading was Hope's first love. Perhaps while she was staying in London, she would acquire something — or someone — to replace that.

★ ★ ★

Over the following days, Hope and her aunt became more relaxed with each other. Hope tried her best to conform to what she felt was required of her, and saved her enthusiasm for when her aunt was out taking tea with her friends or at a concert. During those times, Hope wrote to her parents, made entries in her journal in large, loopy writing, and dreamt of the dinner party which was nearly upon

17

them. She was surprised the Padstocks were not on the invitation list, but had been fascinated when she'd seen the name Beaumont.

A thought struck her. What on earth was she going to wear? She summoned Edna and put the question to her.

'I wondered that myself, my lady, and took the liberty of sponging out the marks on the pale blue silk.'

The doubtful look on Edna's face sent a pulse of panic through Hope. 'You don't think it's suitable, do you?'

'I think your colouring deserves a richer hue.'

'That means you think it's unsuitable, doesn't it?' pushed Hope.

Edna nodded slowly. Then she said, 'I think tea is ready to be served now. I'll have another look through the wardrobe.'

*　*　*

'These scones are delicious,' declared Hope biting into her second one. She

18

caught her aunt's faintly disapproving glance. 'But I certainly couldn't manage a sandwich or a piece of cake as well.' There, she'd redeemed herself. 'I shall have to make sure I can fit into my dress for the dinner.'

'You have some fine dresses, Hope,' began Aunt Constance, 'but I should like to take you shopping for a new one, as this will be your first formal dinner at my home during your stay here. We will visit my dressmaker in Wimpole Street and order a dress for you. It will be designed to accentuate your best features. I thought green silk to bring out the colour of your eyes. What do you say? And then we'll take luncheon at The Dome.'

Hope sprang up and hugged her aunt. 'How generous you are, Aunt. I should love to go shopping with you. Will you purchase something new as well?'

'Goodness me, no. I have several wardrobes full upstairs. In all sizes and colours. Your uncle used to like me to

be well-presented. He always compli-
mented me on my outfits. But now I
have to wear mourning.' She looked
away, but not before Hope noted, with
horror, her aunt's moist eyes.

'Uncle Eustace was lovely. He was a
good match, Aunt.'

That made Constance snort, and the
intimate moment passed. Hope couldn't
wait to tell Edna she was getting a new
outfit. She pictured herself running her
fingers over the silks and velvets. All the
colours of the rainbow, but deeper and
richer. She longed for the outfit to be
finished so she could see if it met her
expectations. Could that be because she
wanted to impress someone? If so,
she wouldn't be telling. She glanced at
her aunt, who appeared to be deep in
thought.

'I still have all Eustace's belongings. I
haven't been able to tell Stevenson to
remove them.'

This was a new, softer side of her
aunt that Hope hadn't seen before.
'May I help in any way, Aunt?'

'Encourage me, my dear. It is pointless holding on to his possessions. I've tried to make a start, but I find it upsetting. I must face the fact that he is gone. Please go upstairs to the second floor; Stevenson will show you the room, and you will see the Herculean task for yourself. I can't think about it anymore today. I will go and rest until dinner.'

Hope wasn't quite sure how she felt about surveying her dead uncle's possessions, but she wanted to help her aunt. She hadn't known Uncle Eustace very well, but she remembered him as being not particularly tall, and somewhat slight. Quite in contrast to her aunt's formidable stature. She wouldn't involve Stevenson just yet, but would first see exactly what there was to be dealt with.

After entering rooms she had never glimpsed before, she finally found one containing all manner of things a gentleman might require. The first objects to catch her attention were the hats piled upon a tallboy. A top hat took her fancy, and without a second thought she placed it on her head. Looking round, she found a long mirror in front of the window, and scrutinised her image in it. She tucked her hair up inside the hat and looked at herself from every angle. If she had a brother, he would surely look like this. Taken with the idea of dressing up, Hope searched the cupboards and found trousers, a shirt, waistcoat and jacket. Having discarded her own garments and thrown them on a chair, she quickly donned her uncle's clothes. They were a little large, but not outrageously so, and were just right for hiding her feminine curves.

She stood in front of the mirror in admiration. She certainly looked different from the picture of herself in a beautiful new gown which she'd imagined just a short time ago. She was aware that men stood and walked differently to women, so set her feet apart and pulled her shoulders back.

'Swagger,' she told herself. She walked round the room, then stood again in front of the mirror. Placing her hands on her hips, she tried to adopt a masculine stance, but was shocked to see the door opening behind her. She turned quickly as Edna appeared.

The maid looked as though she was about to scream. Hope tugged the hat from her head. 'It's only me.'

'Oh, my lady, I thought you were an intruder.' Edna almost ran over to study her. 'You scared the life out of me.'

'Help me change before someone else sees me.' Hope struggled to pull the jacket off, suddenly feeling the need to be rid of the masculine attire. She shouldn't be wearing her dead uncle's clothes. It was appalling behaviour, and if her aunt found out, there would be an awful fuss. 'Come on, please, Edna, help me. Hurry up.' She felt rather faint and breathless, but between them the two young women quickly managed to have Hope dressed in a feminine manner again.

'Ah, that's a relief.' She took a few deep, slow breaths.

Edna smiled. 'It was funny, the way you were altered. You could easily have passed as a man.'

'It was quite convincing, wasn't it? I have to admit, I thought I made rather a handsome fellow.'

'Whatever were you thinking, dressing up like that?'

It was a reasonable question. 'I was thinking that dressed like that, dressed like a man, I could do almost anything I want.' As Hope uttered the words, all sorts of options rushed through her mind. She shook her head to clear it and admonished herself to slow down. She always was one to act first and think later. It was one thing to behave impulsively in front of her parents, but she was now in a grand house in London with her aunt. It would not do at all.

'A very fine man you made, too. I wouldn't mind being seen walking out with you.'

Hope felt as though a huge weight had been lifted from her. 'Really? We could . . . What possibilities . . . No, that's too ridiculous. Come along, Edna. I'm sure you have things to do, and I would like to finish my book before it's time to get ready for dinner.'

Unfortunately, concentration didn't come to Hope. She couldn't get the troublesome thought from her mind that masquerading as a man would offer her numerous opportunities for adventure. What had Edna said? Hope could easily pass as a man, and Edna wouldn't mind being seen walking out with her. With her book open in her lap, Hope let her imagination run wild.

2

Hope was absorbed in the procedure of the fitting which was vastly different from her experiences with her mother. She felt bemused as the dressmaker took complete charge and paraded swatches of materials in various colours before her. She looked to her aunt for guidance, but *she* was sitting in a comfortable chair, engrossed in a fashion article in 'The Queen' magazine. Mindful of Edna's advice about richer colours, she opted for the deeper turquoise, relieved to see the smile of satisfaction on the dressmaker's face. 'Some of the turquoise colours are too blue, but this one is right for you, Lady Hope. I suggest the trimmings are kept to a minimum so as not to detract from your own beauty.'

The laugh Hope was about to explode into was covered with a

discreet cough. Hope realised she was getting quite attracted to the idea of dressing up, be it for enjoyment or something more. While she waited to receive her aunt's approval about the garment, Hope looked around the showroom. Perhaps she would call again and order a couple of modest outfits. She felt she was taking on a new persona. Her stay in London was proving to be more exciting and appealing than she could have wished.

During luncheon, Hope was hardly aware of her plate of mutton and cabbage. Her attention was absorbed by the goings-on around her. If she ate out in a restaurant with her parents, the surroundings were less ornate and the atmosphere quieter than here. Snatches of conversation and laughter reached her, and she wanted to soak everything up. The cutlery clattered down on her plate as she finished her main course. Her aunt, by contrast, slowly ate her portion of pigeon pie and sipped a glass of claret.

Hope turned her attention to her aunt. 'Thank you for my dress, Aunt. I love it.' With happiness, she concentrated on her iced dessert, which slid down her throat with tingling pleasure.

'We should be getting home now,' said Aunt Constance. 'There is a lot to be seen to with regard to the arrangements for the dinner. The time will go by very quickly.'

Hope was reluctant to leave, but it had been a full morning and she'd enjoyed herself. 'It's a pity the Padstocks couldn't attend, isn't it, Aunt? Especially as James Henderson will be there.' Hope couldn't resist the seemingly innocent remark. Perhaps now she would find out the situation between Isabella and James.

'I'm not sure they were aware of his invitation to the event. They had a prior engagement. There will be other opportunities for them to visit if you wish to spend time with the sisters, Hope.'

Although she looked forward to

spending time with Mary and Isabella, Hope wanted to know about the gentlemen who were being invited to dinner in order to meet her. It was time to change the course of the conversation. 'And Mr Beaumont, why is he disliked? If he's such an awful person, why did you invite him, Aunt?' This had been a puzzle to Hope.

Aunt Constance hesitated, as if unsure how to answer the direct questions. 'He knew your uncle, and for some reason they developed — not exactly a friendship, more of a respect, I suppose you could call it. Of course, Eustace had a lot about him to be respectful of, but Beaumont . . . well, he always appeared ill-mannered and discourteous whenever I met him. No quality of diplomacy in him at all.' She clamped her mouth shut and stood up as if anxious to leave.

The story of Mr Beaumont would be hard to unravel. Hope wasn't ready to return to the house just yet, but the thought of writing in her journal about the day and what she knew so far of the dinner guests appealed.

On reaching her room, she picked up her pen and began her journal entry.

I am missing Mama and Papa dreadfully, but Aunt Constance is a dear once she has melted a little. London is always exciting and there are so many agreeable people to meet. I am quite sure Aunt Constance will have me married before my stay is over. James Henderson is young and good-looking, and Mr Beaumont is . . . mysterious.

I am already growing fond of Edna, and she did not appear too alarmed when she found me in Uncle Eustace's clothes. I rather envy gentlemen their freedom from restricting corsets, although I am overjoyed about my new dress.

Next time I will write about The Honourable James Henderson and Mr Beaumont.

★   ★   ★

With Edna's help, Hope pulled on the various layers of underclothing before the beautiful new creation tumbled over her head and fell with a whisper to the ground.

'It's wonderful, my lady,' sighed Edna. 'Such a beautiful colour.'

'I took your advice and chose a rich one. You were right, of course. You have excellent taste. Now, shall we see if my hair will behave itself?'

Hope didn't have as many qualms now about looking in the mirror. She'd got used to her reflection again, and her aunt, the dressmaker and Edna had intimated that she wasn't bad-looking. Her confidence was, if not soaring, at least testing its wings.

'You know Mr Beaumont, don't you, Edna?' The sharp intake of breath didn't go unnoticed by Hope. 'What is the secret surrounding him?'

She watched Edna's frown in the mirror. 'There's no secret as far as I know. He's not a very popular figure. He's too outspoken for a lot of the gentry, begging your pardon.'

Hope dabbed some of her favourite rose scent on her arms and behind her ears. 'I shall find out for myself,' she declared, noticing from her reflection that her eyes were sparkling with mischief. 'I'll tell you all about this evening later, Edna, when I'm preparing for bed.'

There was silence as Hope descended the stairs. She was late, she knew, and anticipated a mild reproof from her aunt. She circulated and made conversation with the guests. Then she felt her pulse racing and grabbed at a chair to steady herself. Turning round slowly, she observed a tall gentleman with curling black hair; unlike most of the other guests, he appeared to make no pretence at enjoying himself or joining in. He merely stood, examining the paintings on the walls, seemingly deep in thought.

Instinctively knowing who he was, Hope approached him. 'Mr Beaumont, how do you do? I'm pleased to make your acquaintance.'

'Are you? Not many people are.' The sound of his voice caused Hope's pulse to quicken. It was deep and resonantly rich, almost musical. Also, she noted that he hadn't flinched when she'd flouted decorum and addressed him first. She trusted her aunt hadn't observed her approach to him. However, she recognised the abrupt manner in which he had answered her.

Hope was only slightly disconcerted. Usually guests at least made an effort to be polite and affable at such occasions, but her parents had friends who were forthright and she had always managed to charm them in some way. She would not be put off. 'You knew my uncle, I understand. I am Hope.'

'I know. And I am Beaumont. Not Mr Beaumont.' With that, he nodded his head to her and walked to a table where he helped himself to a modest amount of whisky.

Hope's mind whirled. She'd been led

to believe he was discourteous and brusque, and he had certainly lived up to his reputation. Had she really thought he'd be any different with her? She shivered slightly. Not from cold, but from anticipation of the evening ahead. How she wished she'd studied her aunt's seating plan. Would she be seated next to Beaumont?

When Stevenson announced that dinner was served, she was escorted to the table by James. Luck was on her side. Taking her place, she looked straight into the mesmeric eyes of the intriguing Beaumont. He stared at her, no smile on his face. Hope sighed to herself. His allure was increasing, and she knew she should put a stop to it, but at that moment she was powerless. She didn't want to put a stop to anything to do with Beaumont until she'd found out more about him and satisfied her curiosity.

'I'm delighted to be here this evening, Lady Hope.' A voice at her side brought her out of her reverie. She turned to face a clean-shaven young gentleman, who introduced himself as James Henderson, and whose face was as sunny and open as Beaumont's was clouded and closed. 'I hope we can get to know each other. Your parents are on the continent, I understand.'

James informed her he had already travelled a good deal, which was possibly why they had never met before. He was keen to apprise Hope of various adventures which could be undertaken whilst abroad. Although she was initially eager to hear what James had to say, Hope was aware of Beaumont's eyes on her throughout the meal. He did not attempt to engage anyone nearby in conversation, and no one appeared anxious or desirous to talk to him. Perhaps what her aunt had said was the whole truth about him: he was rude. But Hope refused to believe that.

She grew fidgety as she listened to James Henderson conversing about shooting parties he'd been on. She found it difficult to stay attentive. His early promise of thought-provoking conversation hadn't lasted long. Half-way through enjoying the turbot, Hope found her gaze wandering to the gentleman who was seated opposite her, and when the succulent roast lamb was served, she merely set about eating it, wondering if Beaumont would engage her in conversation. When the next course of jellied chicken was offered, she declined, as she was becoming aware that her corset was beginning to stifle her.

'Constance.' Beaumont's use of her aunt's Christian name caused a gasp from Stevenson and glares from round the table. This was proving to be a very unusual dinner party. 'What will be done with the leftover food?'

Hope was amazed at his bluntness. She herself had been wondering the same thing. She held her breath as she waited for the conversation to continue.

'I have no idea, Beaumont. Am I expected to oversee the kitchen now? I never set foot in there. If you are so inquisitive about the food from my table, then I'm sure Stevenson can enlighten us.' She raised her eyebrows at Stevenson, and Hope was surprised and delighted to see that her aunt was entertained by the turn of events.

'Some will be used for luncheon tomorrow, Your Grace, and some will be served in the servants' hall.'

'And the rest, Stevenson?' Beaumont persisted. There was no reply. 'It should be parcelled up for the poor.'

'I'm sure the sorbet will be excellent when the poor go to eat it tomorrow.' James guffawed.

'Clearly not the sorbet or other iced desserts, but the meat, fish, bread, fruit and vegetables would be appreciated,' Beaumont said, with an air of impatience.

'Would *you* like a food parcel as well?' James asked.

Beaumont tapped the table. 'I am very well provided for, for which I give thanks. As everyone round this table is aware, my father was a wealthy man who made his money from textiles in the north of England. I do not require a food parcel.'

Hope broke the ensuing silence. 'I for one think it's an excellent idea. What do you say, Aunt Constance? Please could the surplus food be given away?'

'Yes, my dear. Stevenson, see to it.' She nodded at Hope. 'I am quite sure that your late uncle would approve.'

Hope leapt to her feet and rushed over to kiss her aunt on her cheek. 'Oh thank you, Aunt, I'm sure it's a good decision.'

'Really, my dear, a little restraint is required if you wish to ensnare yourself a husband,' Aunt Constance whispered.

Hope capered back to her chair, and breathed a sigh of relief as the guests resumed their conversations. Looking across at Beaumont, she saw that he was gazing at her, and his deep brown eyes held hers for the briefest of moments before she looked away. When she turned back to him, he was looking down at his plate, the glimmer of a smile on his sensuous mouth.

'This dinner party will be the talk of London for weeks to come. Although I must admit to generally being the subject of much conversation amongst the ladies.' The Honourable James Henderson smirked. Hope hid a grin as she thought of James being outdone by a food parcel. 'Still pursuing your hobby, Beaumont?' he asked across the table.

'I have many hobbies, although I don't count country sports amongst them, which I gather are your main pursuit.'

'I'm sure Lady Hope would rather hear about your picture shows than anything I might tell her.'

'Picture shows! What is this hobby of yours, Beaumont?' she asked. He was becoming more and more fascinating. Perhaps now she would find out something about him. At least he must answer her, surely.

'I'm a magic lanternist.' As he imparted this astounding news, his eyes were on her, and it was as if only the two of them were present at the table. Hope blinked rapidly to bring herself back from what must be a flight of fancy. But as she stared at him again, his eyes were still on her, the rest of the guests seemingly ignored. Then she was aware of her aunt's discreet cough and recovered herself.

Her parents had told her about magic lanterns and the shows they had attended. They usually went to see any travel presentations at the town hall. She particularly remembered them telling her about one entitled *The Adventures of David Livingstone*.

'I have recently acquired some excellent old slides. It's a story called *The Ratcatcher*. It's very humorous. It will be part of my next show.' Hope noted that Beaumont's eyes flickered with enjoyment as he talked about his pastime. Was that passion she read in those dark depths?

'Where will that be?' She shouldn't appear so eager, but couldn't help herself.

'At Girton Green. I have been asked to present a number of shows while the fair is there.' He paused as if waiting for a reaction. There was a wall of silence from the guests. Hope wasn't sure why. She supposed a fair was not a respectable venue for the guests presently being entertained at her aunt's house. Perhaps Edna would be able to tell her what went on at fairs, and why she might not be allowed to go. 'The first one is next Wednesday evening at eight.'

Was he inviting her? She couldn't possibly go on her own, but she was tempted.

'You must excuse us, but the ladies will now withdraw.' Constance stood and led the way from the dining room to the drawing room. She took hold of Hope's arm as they walked through. 'Did your dinner companion please you, Hope, dear?'

'Very much. He is handsome, well-educated, intriguing and thought-provoking.' Her heart skipped a beat as she recalled his sensuous lips and the passion in Beaumont's eyes.

'Good. I will ensure there are plenty of opportunities for you to get to know each other better. He is the youngest son of a viscount, a very good family. As you know, Lady Padstock would have him betrothed to Isabella in the blink of an eye.'

It was then Hope knew they were speaking of two different people. She didn't have the slightest curiosity about The Honourable James Henderson, but Beaumont was a different matter. A different kettle of fish, as Edna had said.

Aunt Constance continued, 'It would please me if you would play the piano, and maybe one of the other ladies will sing for us.'

Hope did as requested. She felt herself to be a competent if unexceptional pianist, but performed with enthusiasm. When the gentlemen joined the party, she continued to play; she had no desire to converse with James, and didn't expect Beaumont would wish to talk to her. The other gentlemen seemed as old as her father, and were happy talking amongst themselves. She trusted her aunt hadn't envisaged any of them as possible suitors for her.

'Very accomplished,' a deep voice said from behind, startling her into faltering and playing the wrong notes.

'Hardly; I've lost my place and will have to start again.' She felt flustered with Beaumont so close. 'No, I'll let someone else play for us. I should socialise.' *Whatever is the matter with me?* she wondered as she scurried away to join a group of ladies near the fire.

'Hope, you're looking lovely. Quite the belle of the evening,' remarked a lady who Aunt Constance said knew Hope's parents. 'I trust your mother and father are enjoying the delights of the continent.'

'I haven't heard from them yet,' replied Hope. 'I expect something will come soon. I'm sure they're making the most of the time they have out there.'

Thinking of her parents made Hope miss them more than she'd expected. If her mother had been near, she would have confided her fascination for Beaumont and asked her advice. He was the sort of person her mother would know how to deal with. She would have been captivated by the thought of his magic shows, and wouldn't have hesitated to visit and see for herself. Could Hope do that? She let out a sigh. Not on her own. She couldn't go about London alone, and her aunt would certainly not endorse a visit to entertainment at that particular venue, with or without a chaperone.

Beaumont took his leave a few minutes later, saying he needed some fresh air. Hope was sorry to see him go. He was blunt, but high-minded. Perhaps parcels of food for the poor could be sent out on a regular basis from this house, at least while she was staying here. She shuddered when she thought of Stevenson's face. He'd tried to mask it, but he hadn't concealed his contempt for the idea at all. Thinking of the servants, Hope couldn't wait now to get to her room and unburden herself to Edna. She was developing quite a liking for the young woman.

When all the guests had left the house, Hope approached her aunt. 'Goodnight, Aunt,' she said, kissing her. 'I've had a lovely evening. You're a wonderful hostess. Please excuse me if I retire now.' She gave a little yawn, and made herself walk slowly out of the room until she was able to gallop up the stairs unseen. A spark of an idea had crept into her mind.

3

Just as Hope was despairing of missing Beaumont's magic show, her aunt imparted some news.

'I'm visiting friends this evening. You won't mind entertaining yourself, I'm sure. We are on the committee of the Female Aid Society. You'd be quite bored among us older people, I fear, and I do not wish to discuss the nature of the charity with you.'

Hope knew exactly what her aunt was referring to, as she'd had long conversations with her mother about that particular organisation. It would not be a good idea to let her aunt know, she surmised, and remained tactfully quiet.

'That's fine, Aunt. You go and do your good work. You don't have to spend all your time with me; I've plenty to be going on with. I will continue with my letters, and I've got things to see to in my room.'

As soon as Aunt Constance left the house, Hope picked up her skirts and ran up the stairs, taking them two at a time. She summoned Edna, and the two of them crept along the corridors to Uncle Eustace's room.

Edna held back. 'I don't think I should be here, my lady,' she objected.

'It's all right. You have my permission,' insisted Hope, not wanting the opportunity to slip by. She pulled Edna inside the room and closed the door quietly. 'No one will know we're here. And please do call me Hope now we're on our own. I hate all this formal business. I'm not used to it at home. My family is unconventional and we don't always do the correct thing. As you are aware, my father is an earl, but I have no idea of all the etiquette. My mother was remiss in my education on titles and the correct forms of address.'

'I understand, my la . . . Hope.' Edna

shivered; and not with the cold, Hope was sure.

Quickly, Hope started to strip off. Edna looked shocked and rushed over to her. 'What are you doing?'

'I'm changing into Uncle Eustace's clothes.' She stood in front of the mirror. 'I'm not sure if I should, but I want us to go out tonight. I want to see Beaumont's magic show. The only way I can get there is if we go together. It's at the fair on Girton Green. Do you know it?' In all the excitement, she hadn't asked Edna about the venue.

'Oh dear, it's not a proper area for you to visit. I can't chaperone you, my lady, I mean, Hope.' Edna had turned bright red and her head was twitching. 'I'll lose my job, and then what will I do?'

'You won't, I promise. If anyone finds out, I'll swear I made you do it. I'm sure it will all be perfectly safe. Please agree to accompany me. I'm determined to attend even if I have to go alone.'

Edna hesitated for a moment. 'Very well, I'll go with you; but I'm not happy, not happy at all.'

Hope clasped both her hands. 'Thank you. I'm sure we'll be quite all right if we're together.' She rummaged in the cupboards and found what she was looking for. With Edna's unenthusiastic help, she finally presented herself in front of the mirror, and the two young women gasped as a man and a woman were reflected in front of them.

'It's very lifelike, I'll give you that.' Edna grinned. 'You *do* make a convincing man. If I didn't know it was you, Hope, I'd think you were a man. If you know what I mean.'

Hope giggled and Edna joined in. 'It's not quite right. I need a moustache or beard.'

'You can't grow one! Perhaps we could fashion a moustache.'

'Yes, cut a piece from my hair and let us see what we can make.' Hope took the hat off and pulled out a pin, releasing a tress of hair.

'Are you sure? I will need a sizeable piece.'

'Yes, yes, cut some off.'

'I will fetch some scissors from below stairs, as your embroidery scissors are not suitable for the job.' Within minutes, Edna had returned, snipped off a bundle of strands, and was struggling to tie the lock to make a moustache. 'It's impossible. It will never look real. I am quite sure you can pass as a clean-shaven young man.'

'I suppose so.' Hope studied herself doubtfully in the mirror again. 'You will have to cut the rest of my hair.'

'Oh, no, my lady, that will never do.'

'I will have to remove my hat, and then my disguise will be uncovered. If you cut it unfashionably long then you will still be able to pin it up when I am back as myself. If you add some of the false hairpieces which Mama insisted I bring with me, then no one will ever know. Only you.'

'You mean you want it like The Honourable James Henderson's hair.

He wears his hair rather long, although I think it suits him.'

'Exactly like his. Now, come along, Edna, let's get on with it.' The maid looked bemused as she carried out her instructions.

As her long tresses fell to the floor, Hope wondered if her impulsive nature would one day lead her into terrible trouble. Edna's hairdressing skills were limited, and it took a while for the two young women to be satisfied with the result.

'There, that doesn't look too bad, does it? With and without my hat, I think I look quite presentable. Now we've got to find something for you to wear.'

'I'm not putting on his Lordship's things,' demurred Edna. 'It's one thing you doing it, but quite another for me.'

'I agree. Let's go back to my room and see what we can find.'

'First I must clear up all the hair. We don't want anyone finding out what we've been up to.'

* ★ ★

At last they were ready to creep downstairs and let themselves out into the street. As they kept to the darker corners, no one paid them any attention, and they gradually became bolder. Hope adopted a mannish air and lowered her voice, and Edna almost skipped along in her borrowed costume.

'Are you sure you know the way, Edna?'

Edna nodded vigorously. 'Oh yes, madam — I mean, Hope, I mean — oh dear, what do I call you?'

Hope giggled before considering this important question. 'Well,' she said, at last, 'my surname is Richmond, so I suppose I could be Richard. Could you manage to call me that?'

'Yes, Richard,' said Edna, solemnly. 'See, I can! It's quite a long walk, Richard, but I know all the short cuts. And I think I'm doing very well at calling you Richard, Richard,' she continued, before breaking into laughter.

Growing in confidence, they made their way to Girton Green. Hope was almost open-mouthed with wonder as they walked past all the shows. There were fortune-tellers, prize fighters and medicine men, amongst other novelties. She would have liked to slow their pace and enjoy the atmosphere, which was full of life, but she didn't want to miss Beaumont's performance.

As they arrived at the marquee advertising the magic lantern show, Hope pulled Edna into the shadows. 'You do know we might bump into Beaumont, don't you?' Edna nodded. 'There will be no reason for us to worry about that, though; he will not recognise you, and he will certainly not know who I am.'

Hope felt a rush of exhilaration as the surroundings engaged her senses. There appeared to be none of the good manners of the society she was used to; everyone was talking loudly and there was a lot of jostling. A man abruptly fell against her arm, and she felt the coarseness of his clothes as she instinctively put out a hand to steady him. He laughed in her face, and she recoiled slightly at the sour odour of his breath before he went on his way.

Edna nudged her, and together they looked at the pugilists getting ready for a bout of fighting. Hope was horrified, but couldn't take her eyes off the men who were dressed — or rather, undressed, it seemed to her — in their underwear. She swallowed hard and gripped Edna's arm, forcing them towards the marquee entrance.

The first hurdle was gaining admission without paying, as neither of them had money with them. It hadn't occurred to Hope that there would be a charge for admission. Next time, she must remember. Next time! That was something to think about, but for now she must concentrate on the present. From the main entrance, Hope spotted a gap in a curtain, dragged Edna through it, and nodded to some spare seats at one side. Edna headed towards them, and Hope followed, letting out a breath that they'd got this far undetected.

They sat bemused, unsure what to expect. The place was filled with people conversing loudly. Raucous laughter caused her to seek its source, and in so doing, she noted everyone looked happy and carefree.

Various smells assailed her nostrils, from alcohol and tobacco to the soup and fried fish which pervaded the marquee from the stalls outside. Her mouth watered. Then Hope became aware of a presence she couldn't account for; but if the prickling feeling on her skin was anything by which to judge, Beaumont was close by. She dared not turn her head, and stared fixedly ahead, edging closer to Edna, who put her hand timidly on Hope's arm. As soon as the mellifluous voice was heard, the audience quietened and took notice. The voice commanded attention with its hypnotic intensity. Of course, Hope knew immediately to whom it belonged.

She was entranced. There was an air of expectancy as the marquee flap was closed and the area darkened. Then a sudden bright light appeared on the canvas. Images were projected, and the audience was silenced as the show began. The first story which Beaumont told alongside the pictures had a moral theme, but the second was an animated comedy called *The Ratcatcher*, as promised at the dinner. Hope giggled when the rat dived into the sleeping man's mouth, and received a sharp nudge in the ribs from Edna. 'You're a gentleman,' her maid whispered, 'you may not giggle.' They both tried to stifle another fit of laughter. Then, much to Hope's consternation, there were boos and hisses as an upside-down image appeared on the screen. She didn't want to witness any fights which weren't on the programme. As she looked around a little fearfully, she noticed the smiles which tempered the jeering.

The next images were about travel, and there was no narration from Beaumont as the pictures were accompanied by a piece on the piano. Hope was glad of a short respite from listening to Beaumont so she could ponder on what she'd seen and heard. It was enchanting, and she felt as if she were in a magic world — which, of course, she was, she realised. This time she managed to hide her burst of delight.

At the end of the show, there was much applause, and the two young women joined in enthusiastically.

'I think we ought to leave now, Richard,' Edna said, as she stood up.

'Yes, we must make our exit without delay.' Squeezing through the crowds, Hope tried to stop herself from apologising, but also to keep her eye on Edna. As she glanced back, she bumped into someone and heard a clatter of glass.

'My goodness!'

It was Beaumont. She had knocked some of his slides to the floor. Being this near to him, she was aware he smelt clean and fresh, not of alcohol or tobacco even though she knew he took whisky. Desperately wanting to look into his eyes, she dared not in case he recognised her. But why would he? Then she remembered he'd extended a tenuous invitation to her to be here. Briefly, she pondered the thought that he had been looking out for her. That was a ridiculous notion. Taking a deep breath, she stopped herself from speaking immediately, and when she did try out her manly voice she found she was also unexpectedly speaking with an accent.

'I am veery soory. 'Ere, allow me to 'elp you.' Even to herself, Hope sounded as if she'd had a bump on the head.

'No, please, you've done enough damage.' But Hope was already bending down and their bodies collided.

When she was upright again, she was conscious of Beaumont regarding her closely, the one thing she'd tried to avoid. His eyes registered puzzlement when they caught hers, and Hope scurried outside, longing to escape without further mishap.

Out in the fresh air, Hope collapsed against Edna and laughed. Tears streamed down her face. 'Did you hear me?'

'I did, my . . . Richard.' Edna started laughing as well. It was only when Hope realised people were staring and making comments that she managed to pull herself together. 'It eez time for us to go 'ome, my dear. Come along.' She tucked Edna's arm through hers and tried to walk in a masculine way without appearing to be hurrying.

Hope felt the evening had been a success. She'd ventured out into London as a man in the company of a servant, and had visited a magic lantern show where she'd passed herself off as a stranger to someone she'd recently been seated near at a formal dinner. Quite an achievement, she told herself.

'Do I know you?'

Hope's self-congratulation choked in her throat as she looked up into the dark eyes of Beaumont. His mocking look put her off-balance, and she leant heavily against Edna, who obviously wasn't expecting to have to catch her mistress. The two of them toppled towards Beaumont, who put out his arms to steady them both.

'I trust you two haven't been drinking too much. The ale they sell here is very potent.' Again, Hope was aware of his magnetic eyes burning into hers. She knew if she opened her mouth to speak again now, she would reveal herself to him. His eyes narrowed and he inclined his head towards Hope. 'Have you a sister with whom I'm acquainted, I wonder? You look like someone I know, and I smell her scent on your skin, too.'

'I expect that's me,' spoke out Edna.

'I like a nice rose scent. It's common enough.' She tugged at Hope's sleeve. 'Come along, Richard, it's time we were going home.' She nodded at Beaumont. 'It's my distant cousin's first visit to England from France, and he's anxious to take in the wonders of London.'

'Come back here on Saturday afternoon, and I shall give you both an insight into the magic lantern shows.'

Edna pulled at Hope's arm and tried to entice her away, but she was reluctant to leave the gentleman who had created feelings in her she had never known before. On the one hand, she felt she had to trust her aunt's judgment — at least to some extent — and avoid him; but at the same time, some invisible thread drew her to him. She felt on the upsurge of an adventure and knew one false move could put an abrupt end to it. His eyes had held hers, and for a moment Hope thought he'd recognised her. Also, she'd made the mistake of not washing off her scent. Most gentlemen only smelt of tobacco. Whatever anyone said about him, someone like Beaumont would never put up with a shameless woman who pretended to be someone she was not. She was sure he had a strict code of what was acceptable.

When they had collided, a spark of something had run through her whole body. *Had he felt it as well?* she speculated. With her eyes still on him, Hope wondered what she could say or do to prolong this meeting; but Edna was tugging at her, and reluctantly she gave in to her maid's unspoken pleas.

Coming to her senses when they had put a short distance between them and Beaumont, Hope quailed at the thought she had acted inappropriately. Although now her legs couldn't carry her away fast enough, with Beaumont's invitation ringing in her head, she knew she would be returning to this very place. The thing of which she wasn't certain was if she would be returning as Richard or Hope.

4

Last time I promised to make a journal entry about the two gentlemen I encountered at Aunt Constance's dinner. These are my thoughts. I wish I could write more expressively like Charles Dickens. Maybe one day I will do as the Brontë sisters did and send off some work to a publisher using a masculine pseudonym — Richard, perhaps. I find it impossible to believe that I dared dress as a man and fool everyone.

The Honourable James Henderson is a perfectly decent and pleasant young man. He is clean-shaven with a 'good head of hair', as Papa would say. I think he is slightly younger than I am, possibly twenty-two or twenty-three. He enjoys shooting parties on big estates. I am unsure why he is regarded as a good match for Isabella by Lady

Padstock, as he is the youngest son, thus will inherit little. The Padstocks are very rich (how vulgar of me to mention it) so maybe marriage into a good family is all they are looking for.

Now to Beaumont. How baffling that he chooses not to use a title. When I find out the reason, I will note it down here in my journal. How to describe him? His age is difficult to judge, but I think he may be thirty-five or there-abouts. Why has he never married? Maybe he has. His black hair curls over his collar and his beard and moustache are neatly trimmed. His shoulders are broad as he fills his coat and he is taller than I, but not by too much. I would only need to stretch up a little for my lips to reach his. I am remembering his eyes which are deep pools to drown in. What nonsense this is. Anyone would think I am in love with him. Have I fallen under his spell? I will write no more.

* * *

The days went by unbearably slowly. Hope tried to fill them as best she could, but was getting increasingly impatient at the thought of returning to the fair on Saturday. As she tried to unravel her reasons, she wasn't sure if it was the thought of meeting Beaumont again, or viewing the magic lantern shows, or the whole new life which was opening up before her. Then came news she did not want to hear.

'I've asked Edna to help me with my wardrobe. It's time I sorted through the vast array of clothing I have. After the meeting about the Female Aid Society, I feel sure they can be put to good use.'

'I could assist you, Aunt,' replied Hope.

'It's not your place, dear. But you being here has helped me to see that I must look to the future instead of remaining in the past.' Constance smiled at her niece. 'Perhaps you can help with sorting some of your uncle's books. There are some volumes he preferred not to put into the library, as they were special to him. Most of them are travel books, I believe, so they may appeal to you. You might like to keep them, or at least read them whilst you are here. You must go and see what you can find.'

'I'd like that,' said Hope. Then she added, 'I found Uncle Eustace's room as you suggested. It's full of appealing things.' She daren't add anything more, except to ask when her aunt and Edna would be engaged in the sorting of her outfits.

'On Saturday afternoon. We've nothing arranged for that time, and it would suit me well.'

Hope's mood plummeted. Without Edna to accompany her, it seemed she was thwarted, unless . . . Oh goodness, did she have the courage to return to the fair on her own? If she did, she would have to go as Richard, because she would have no chaperone. The thought caused her heart to beat faster, and she was sure her face was as pink as the roses on Aunt Constance's table.

Her mind raced along with her heart as she tried to envisage the situation. First of all, she must make sure she had the necessary attire for her proposed outing; and to do that, she would need to enter her uncle's room. Now, of course, she had the perfect excuse.

'I will go and look at Uncle's books right away if that is convenient to you.'

'Please do, my dear. Maybe Stevenson can clear the room soon. I feel I am ready to oversee that undertaking too.'

Hope didn't skip out of the room or run up the stairs. She felt as though she was deceiving her aunt. She had been brought up to be open and honest and talk about her undertakings to her parents. Was it dishonest of her to remove some of her uncle's clothes and to use them to deceive her aunt further by going out in secret?

Back in the room, her negative thoughts quickly disappeared, and she was soon lost in another world as she curled up in her uncle's well-upholstered chair with a book open in her lap.

Hope sighed as she snapped the book shut. It had taken her on a journey to the sorts of places she thought her parents would be visiting. She had especially enjoyed the section on Paris, which sounded the most romantic city. If only one day she would have the chance to experience all it offered, just as her parents would do. She felt guilty when envy crossed her mind. How could she be jealous of her own parents? They deserved to be touring abroad, and she was certain a letter would arrive from them soon. Her aunt had invited her to take some of the books, and she scooped up an armful, together with some of Uncle Eustace's clothes. When she touched the outfit she'd worn to the fair, a tremor of anticipation ran through her. Hope returned to her own room, put the books on a shelf, and found a hiding place for Richard's clothes.

★　★　★

On Saturday, Hope woke early and lay in bed thinking of the day ahead. When Edna arrived to help her get dressed, she decided she wouldn't raise the subject of the fair. That way, the maid wouldn't be put in a difficult situation if questions were asked.

How she managed to get through breakfast and luncheon, she didn't know. She certainly had no appetite, but tried to force a small amount of food down so her aunt would not think she was coming down with something.

At last her aunt said, 'You will have some time to yourself today, Hope. I've asked Edna to assist me, as you might remember.'

'Yes, I do.' As if she would forget that. She gave her aunt time to ensconce herself upstairs before she followed. Once inside her room, Hope changed into Richard's clothes and sat breathlessly on the bed. Hearing what she thought was an exchange between her aunt and Edna, and a door closing, Hope took a chance and peeped out onto the landing. All seemed clear; she descended the stairs, opened the front door and fled along the pavement, not daring to look behind her.

When she'd turned the corner, she slowed down and put on her best swagger. People passed her, but no comment was made, and no one looked strangely at her. Feeling confident, she peered into shop windows and ambled along. There was no hurry. Her new awareness of fashion swayed her into stopping at one particular window. The dress she viewed was utterly elegant, and she spent a long time surveying it. Then she knew she'd made a mistake. Why would a young man be staring into a dress shop? As she turned away abruptly, a carriage drew up outside the shop. And out of it stepped Isabella Padstock. They stood facing each other, and Hope knew she should do something. Raise her hat. That was it, but as she reached up to do so, she knew her face would be in full view.

Thinking and acting quickly, she put

one hand up to her hat and, with the other, opened the door of the shop. Isabella glanced briefly at her before she swept inside, making no sign of recognition. Again, Hope had gone undetected, but she felt she had to put distance between herself and Isabella as quickly as possible.

Marching along the road at a pace, Hope could identify none of the landmarks she'd remembered from her expedition with Edna. She was well and truly lost. Then she recalled her initial ideas when she'd considered the freedom gentlemen had. She could, of course, ask the way to the fair.

With her sudden new-found confidence she enquired of another gentleman the way to the fair; to her horror, he offered to accompany her, as he too was going to see the magic lantern show. Now she had to act the part of a man for a considerable time. As soon as the gentleman discovered his companion was French and on a visit to London, he talked about the sights they passed. Hope shrugged and muttered the occasional *non* or *oui*. On arrival at their destination they parted company and Hope sighed with relief as she took a seat. All she wanted to do was enjoy the show and listen to Beaumont's storytelling.

'Ah, I wondered if you'd return for today's show.' Beaumont was at her side. 'Is your cousin not with you?'

'My cousin? Yes, I mean, no, she was unavailable so I came alone.' Hope longed for Beaumont to talk to her further, but at the same time she was aware that he might detect that she was neither French nor a man.

'I remember her calling you 'Richard'. Delighted you returned. I promised you and your cousin an insight into the magic shows. Please come with me, and I will demonstrate the order to place the slides into the lantern. They have to be inserted like *this*. I will stand at the front and tell the story whilst you manoeuvre the slides, if that is agreeable to you.' He appeared in a remarkably good mood as he chuckled and beamed at her.

Hope's hands trembled. How should she respond? Should she simply flee and never return? But the thought of listening to Beaumont's harmonious voice and being in close proximity to him decided her. As she fumbled with the first of the slides at the start of the show, she wondered how she had managed to get herself into such an awful predicament. Papa and Mama often said she was impulsive, but they had made no attempt to curb her spontaneity. She supposed that if she had been one of Lady Padstock's daughters she would be safe at home sewing or at the dressmaker.

The lights were dimmed, and gradually she relaxed and was able to concentrate on putting the slides in and out at the correct moments. She began to enjoy herself. Listening to Beaumont, she was transported, and almost squeaked with delight each time one of the slides she'd inserted was magnified upon the screen. She found she was working in harmony with the man who now filled her thoughts. That he trusted her with this responsibility filled her with pleasure, and she didn't want to let him down. When the story ended, the audience applauded rapturously. Beaumont returned to her side.

'A resounding success, Richard. The next images are accompanied by my pianist, but at the end of the show I am going to my club to eat, and would be pleased if you would accompany me. I would like to show my appreciation for your help.'

Is that how gentlemen behaved? Inviting someone they barely knew to their club? And how was she to evade the invitation?

'My cousin, you met, Edna, ees, I mean she ees expecting me 'ome when the show is over.'

'That is a pity. Another time, perhaps.'

Hope couldn't concentrate on the pictures of faraway places she had only ever read about in books. All she could think about was Beaumont. It would be illuminating to visit a gentlemen's club, but she wasn't ready for an incident of that sort quite yet. She felt slightly sick and dizzy. What a fool she was. What had she expected to gain by coming to this unsuitable place?

At the end of the show, she wanted to steal away; but it was as though Beaumont had been keeping an eye on her, and he was by her side as soon as she stood up.

'I have a request to make. I am putting on a show on the twenty-first at St Martin's church hall, in aid of a very worthwhile charity, and need some assistance. It would simply be inserting the slides as you have done today. I would welcome your help as would the beneficiaries. It is for the Female Aid Society. A worthy cause.'

'Yes, yes, I'll be there.' Hope fled from him before another word was said. It was only when she was some streets away that she was able to stop and allow herself to take some deep breaths. She was falling deeper and deeper into a horrible pit of deception. To let the Female Aid Society down would be terrible, but she might not be able to attend if her aunt had other plans. And then it occurred to her that her aunt might also be attending the charitable function.

Arriving at Aunt Constance's house, Hope was unable to bring herself to use the front entrance and instead crept through the kitchen door and made her way silently to her rooms using the servants' stairs. Thankfully she didn't meet a soul until she opened her door.

'Hope! Richard! Where have you been? I've been worried and have lied to your aunt. She wanted to know your whereabouts and I told her you are suffering from a headache. She almost insisted on coming in to see you so I told her you were asleep and it was best not to disturb you.'

'Thank you, Edna. I'm sorry. I didn't

tell you where I was going because I didn't want to involve you. But I see I have done worse than that. I have put you in an intolerable position and I am very sorry.'

'Did you not think your absence would be noticed?'

'I didn't think, Edna. Please forgive me.' She took the young maid's hands in her own.

'Of course I do, but I am worried. Your aunt might send me away and my family depends on me. I can't let them down.'

'I understand and I'm truly sorry.'

Edna gave her a smile. 'You'd get away with anything. Let me help you take those clothes off and let's return you to being Hope. I prefer her to Richard.'

As Edna busied herself Hope told her about the afternoon's events and about the invitation to help at the charity event.

Then, transformed to herself, Hope went downstairs to speak to her aunt.

She felt most contrite as she entered the room.

'Hope, dear, are you feeling better? You do look pale. Come and sit by me.' Constance beckoned her near.

'I'm much improved. Did you have a nice afternoon?'

'Edna and I have progressed well and have managed to put aside a quantity of clothing for the charity in which I'm involved. It's a very worthwhile cause and it's probably time you knew what it was all about as you might find yourself involved with it in the coming weeks.'

Her aunt looked decidedly uncomfortable and Hope, taking pity on her, whispered, 'Mother talked to me about the Female Aid Society so I've an outline of an idea as to what it entails. And if I can be of assistance to you in any way, please let me know. I shall be only too happy to help.'

Hope was rewarded with a sigh of relief from Constance. 'Thank you,' she said. 'Now I have some other news. Isabella visited briefly while you were resting and there is something I would like to discuss with you.'

So Isabella *had* recognised her and had come running to tell stories to Aunt Constance. Whatever could she say in her defence? She wouldn't deceive her any more. She would tell the truth whatever the consequences.

5

What Hope had feared hadn't presented itself and Isabella had merely
visited with a view to imparting the
news that she was having some
fashions made up for herself and her
suspicion that Hope would like to hear
about them. Constance had generously
invited her niece to order some more
outfits, but she was adamant that she
would pay for them herself.

'Father gave me an allowance for the
time he and Mama are away and I had
already decided to re-visit your dressmaker and choose some things from
her.'

'That would be an excellent idea. I
shall accompany you.'

'Dear Aunt, you've been good in spending time with me, but I know you've
things of your own to occupy yourself
with. May Edna come with me?'

'A servant? Go with you to the dressmaker? Why, Hope, that's a little . . . ' Constance had been rendered speechless. 'Very well,' she said at last. 'If that's what you want. Take my carriage.'

* * *

Hope hid a smile as she watched Edna marvel at the showroom. Several times she put out her hands to finger the materials, but didn't quite connect with them. 'Edna, what colours should I have this time? This red is beautiful.'

Edna coughed discreetly and Hope saw a conspiratorial look pass between her maid and the dressmaker. 'I think the *ruby* red shot silk would suit your skin tones, my lady.'

Hope gathered a handful of the material, enjoying its coolness. She held it up to her face and regarded herself in the mirror. If Beaumont saw her in this what would he think? Would he be spellbound by her? Everything she thought about lately was connected

81

with the gentleman with no title. As she thought about her term for him, she smiled and was surprised by the gentleness her rounded cheeks and soft eyes gave her features. 'I like it,' she said at last. 'And what about the dove grey? With perhaps purple trimmings? How would that be? Oh, and I think this golden coloured material is perfect for a ball gown. If you two agree with my choice of fabrics, we could select some styles now.'

The three of them were engrossed for a fair time examining designs, but at last they were all agreed as to what Hope would purchase.

'I'd like to look around,' declared Hope, doing just that. Edna stood to one side until her mistress approached and asked, 'Do you like this, Edna?' She was holding a pretty white fan with an intricate floral pattern upon it.

'It's beautiful, my lady.' Edna eyes shone. 'It will go very well with the ruby dress you're having made.'

Hope handed it to the dressmaker

and continued looking around the shop. She picked up a moiré ribbon sash in a delicate shade of yellow. It reminded her of a primrose. The thought made her happy. 'I'll take this and the fan with me,' she said.

Back in the carriage, Hope gave the wrapped fan to Edna. 'This is for you. Thank you for your help in choosing the dresses.' She was careful not to mention their illicit outing as she didn't want the maid to think she was giving her a bribe to keep quiet.

'Oh, my lady, I shouldn't take that. It's my job to help you and being taken to a proper dressmaker's is more than I have ever dared dream of. You'll be giving me ideas above my station.' Nevertheless, Hope was pleased to note that Edna kept hold of the packet. She trusted her aunt would be as happy when presented with the ribbon sash. Hope felt sure it was not too soon for her aunt to be edged out of mourning.

★   ★   ★

Quite excited at the thought of giving her aunt the gift, Hope could barely contain her impatience until dinner. She decided to write in her journal to help the time pass.

In spite of a wonderful time shopping with Edna, at the back of my mind is the dread I feel as the twenty-first creeps ever closer. I have said I will, as Richard, help Beaumont with the charity magic lantern show. My two biggest fears are that I will not be able to attend because Aunt Constance has made other arrangements for me or, worse still, that I am able to keep my promise and Aunt Constance is also there. Then there is the fear that I will be found out. How did I manage to get myself into such an awful muddle? The situation could not be worse. Edna is here now telling me it is time for dinner. I am at least optimistic my aunt will like her gift.

★ ★ ★

'Ah, Hope, dear. Come and sit down and tell me all about your outing and then I will tell you about my visitor.'

'It was wonderful, Aunt. We chose the most superb material . . . '

'We being?'

'Edna and I. We chose ruby red, dove grey with purple trimmings and a golden material.'

'A word of advice, my dear. Familiarity with the servants is to be avoided. It may cause complications. Now tell me about the designs of your new dresses. Did you choose the latest styles?'

Hope chatted happily to her aunt in spite of feeling a little vexed at the warning she had been given. She produced the gift which she had carefully wrapped and tied with a yellow ribbon.

Her aunt opened the package and exclaimed on seeing the contents, 'It's a beautiful colour. Eustace adored primroses. I will wear it in memory of him. Thank you, my dear, it was most thoughtful of you.'

As the meal progressed, Hope's mind wandered yet again to her predicament. It wasn't in her nature to deceive anyone let alone someone she loved. Should she tell her aunt everything? No, she would be sent away with no possibility of seeing Beaumont again and that she couldn't bear.

'I received a visitor today. Beaumont.'

Hope nearly fell off her chair. She had been daydreaming, picturing him when their eyes had met after she had knocked his slides to the floor. She took a deep breath.

'He asked for your assistance and I gladly gave it. He is giving a magic lantern show in support of the Female Aid Society on the twenty-first and has need of a pianist. He asked if you would be available and if I would give permission for you to attend. The venue is a church hall, somewhat different from the last venue he mentioned, so I have agreed to his request on your behalf. I hope that is acceptable to you. I will be accompanying you.'

Hope could barely speak. Beaumont had asked for her help. She felt light-headed at the thought. Was he interested in her as more than a pianist? Surely there must be numerous people willing to play the piano for him and a good cause. But it wasn't just that. Her light-headedness increased when she thought about him asking Richard for *his* help as well. Whatever was she to do?

'Hope, Hope, what is the matter?'

'Nothing is the matter. I am simply astounded that you are willing to allow me to help that man. You do not approve of him.'

'He has his defects. One also wonders why at his age he hasn't yet married and why he refuses to use his title, Mister. It is exceedingly odd. You are correct. I do not approve of him in many ways, but I approve of the good work he does which redeems him to a certain extent.'

'I see.' She could think of nothing else to say.

'I do believe you are suffering from a malady. I will ask the cook to prepare you a reviving herbal drink. Go to your room and Edna will bring it to you. I will send for the doctor tomorrow if you are still as ashen as now.'

'I am fine, Aunt, there is no need to worry.'

'There is every need to worry. You are in my care and I will let nothing harm you. Stevenson, send for Edna to help my niece to her room.'

* * *

As she lay on the bed Hope pondered her predicament. If only she had someone to share her worries with. Should she confide in Edna?

'Here we are, Hope. If you sit up and drink this I'm sure you'll feel a lot better. I can't imagine what came over you. You appeared perfectly well on our outing.'

'Sit down, Edna.' Hope patted the bed. 'I have done something terrible and it is only worry which made me seem poorly. I feel the need to unburden myself and you are my only real friend here in London.'

'Oh, my lady, I can't be your friend. We are from different worlds.'

'I like you and trust you. If you regard me in the same way then we are friends.'

'Whatever would Her Grace say!'

Hope sipped at the hot, sweet-smelling drink. 'She would warn me not to be familiar with a servant.' The two women smiled at each other and then Hope told Edna of her adventure and how she was to be at the show as both Richard and Hope.

'My lady! Whatever will you do?'

'We must think of a plan. You could go dressed as me.'

'I can't play the piano and we look nothing alike.'

'I mean dressed as me when I am Richard. We are the same size.' They looked at each other and laughed. 'I am absurd. You are a head shorter than me and our colouring is quite different.'

'I will go and tell Mr Beaumont that my cousin Richard is indisposed.'

'Then who will insert and remove the slides? I am afraid I have ruined the show. I could go as Richard and another pianist could take my place, but Aunt Constance will be there. It is all too complicated. It is impossible. Thank you for trying to help. Please leave me now. I will try to sleep.' As she closed her eyes she remembered what she had written in her journal. 'The situation could not be worse.' It was decidedly worse and there was no easy solution.

6

When Hope awoke, she stretched and felt content. Her aunt had liked her ribbon sash gift and she had some new dresses to look forward to wearing. On what occasions she wasn't sure. Then she sat up abruptly, causing her head to spin and a dull ache to snake across her head and neck. She was remembering the dilemma regarding herself, Richard and Beaumont. Of course, a simple solution would be to put away the masculine clothes she had acquired and dismiss Richard forever. Beaumont had no way of tracing him or connecting him with her. That was it! A good solution.

It was then that Hope recollected her resolution to tell the truth whatever the consequences. Well, if she didn't meet Beaumont as Richard, she would not be lying to him. But it was an unsatisfactory situation. She owed Beaumont the decency of an apology for Richard's absence. She would have to dress as Richard, seek Beaumont out and explain that the twenty-first was an unsuitable date. Feeling calmer with the decision made, Hope took the opportunity of a little more sleep.

The next time she opened her eyes, Edna was in her room drawing back the drapes.

'Good morning,' Hope said. 'I feel a lot better today. And look, the sun is shining.'

'Hope, Her Grace has decided to take breakfast in the dining room this morning.'

'My goodness, I'd better hurry.'

★ ★ ★

With Aunt Constance overseeing household arrangements, Hope was at a loose end. In her bedroom, she took out Richard's clothes from the back of the cupboard she'd hidden them in. Now was the perfect opportunity to call off the appointment with Beaumont. Dressed as Richard, she felt more assertive and was sure she could accomplish her objective. That was until she realised she had no idea where to find Beaumont! Her aunt would be the only person who could tell her and she couldn't approach her in that respect. It would only lead to complicated questions. In her uncle's clothes, Hope set off in the direction of the fair thinking she would find someone to ask there.

Frustrated to find the main entrance of the marquee closed, Hope tried to find a different way in. A voice called, 'Monsieur, how good to see you this fine morning.'

Hope held her breath and turned around. It was the gentleman who had accompanied her to the fair. He might well come to her rescue. She returned his greeting. Then she noted with agitation that the man was beginning to walk away. 'Did you enjoy the show?'

'It was a fine example of a magic

lantern programme. You were the projectionist, were you not? You did well, the pictures synchronised perfectly with the narration. Are you here for a further performance?'

'Non, I am looking for something.' Hope could not bring herself to tell another lie, so she changed it to, 'I should say I am looking for someone. Beaumont. Do you know if he's inside?'

'Let's find out.'

Hope followed the gentleman through a small gap in the canvas she hadn't noticed before and stood in the tent which appeared very different without crowds of people laughing and chattering and filling it out. She glanced round thinking how wonderful it would be to see Beaumont. After her explanation, she would put away Richard's clothes forever.

'Good morning, Richard. How are you today?' Beaumont's voice reached Hope, but hard as she searched, she couldn't see him. 'Over here, by the stage.'

Hope looked and there he was looking wonderfully elegant. She hurried towards him and blurted out the reason for her seeking him out. When he seemed amused rather than put out, Hope nearly stamped her foot until she remembered that was not very masculine behaviour. 'I thought I should let you know. No doubt you will be able to replace me. The person I came in with could 'elp you out per'aps, *monsieur*.' With glee, Hope noticed Beaumont's eyes darken and the smile on his mouth faltered. There, she'd given him a title whether he wanted one or not! Not wanting to be at the receiving end of his wrath, Hope retraced her footsteps and left, pausing only to bid farewell to the gentleman who had assisted her entry.

On the way home, Hope wished that perhaps she hadn't acted quite so impulsively. If only she'd been more regretful, she could have spent more time with Beaumont. But she couldn't have kept up the pretence, she was sure, especially in view of the fact she felt ashamed now to be dressed in Uncle Eustace's clothes.

★　★　★

When she arrived home, Hope tore off the clothes she'd been wearing and pulled the dress which had been her mother's over her head. If only Mama were here. Inhaling the faint vestiges of her mother's scent from the material, she drew a blank page from her escritoire and began to unburden herself in a letter.

Dearest Mama, dearest Papa,

Thank you for your package from Florence. I am very pleased to have received it as I was impatient to hear news from you. The drawings you sent are exquisite and I would like to have the one of the cathedral framed when we are home again. You are very talented, Mama.

Pisa sounds delightful. And now you are travelling to Naples and going to see Pompeii. Is Vesuvius still smouldering? I hope to visit the British Museum and see the exhibition there if I can persuade Aunt Constance to go with me.

She has been very kind and is introducing me to London society. We are great friends with Lady Padstock, Mary and Isabella. I am probably rather an embarrassment being unmarried at my age, but Aunt Constance is doing her best to rectify this. She has set her sights on James Henderson, more correctly The Honourable James Henderson. He is personable, but I am sure there are other potential suitors whom I would prefer, and Lady Padstock has high expectations of him for Isabella.

Hope paused and chewed the end of her fountain pen. Should she mention Beaumont? No, not in a letter. She would tell her mother everything when they were together again. As she thought of him her heart beat a little faster and she felt giddy with joy as she considered meeting him on the twenty-first. It was only a short while away. She continued with her letter.

Aunt Constance has accepted a request on my behalf. I am to play the piano at a magic lantern show for charity. I feel sure better pianists are available, but I am happy to oblige for a good cause. Papa, you need not be concerned with the following. I am having some dresses made in the latest style which is very exciting. Also we have been invited to a ball. I believe Aunt Constance will chaperone me as she feels that it is time for her to rejoin society after two years of mourning. She accepts invitations for tea and attends committee meetings, but this will be her first ball without Uncle Eustace. And James Henderson will be there which delights her. I am afraid I will let her down as etiquette at balls is far too complicated. Mama, why did you not educate me better?

I have forgotten to tell you about Edna. She is my maid although she has not been a lady's maid before. Without the experience she is perhaps not as competent as Ruth, but I like her very much. I do think of Ruth and trust that her parents have recovered from the influenza. I will write a simple letter to her and expect she can remember all I taught her. I gave her some of the books I had as a child to take home and I'm sure she will enjoy them. Aunt Constance has given me the run of the library here, but also let me look through Uncle Eustace's special books which are mainly travel accounts and include Pictures from Italy by Charles Dickens. It is fascinating.

Yesterday Aunt Constance told me that she would like you, Papa, to have Uncle Eustace's pocket watch and it is now in my care. It will be a lovely reminder of your dear brother-in-law.

Hope stopped again. She didn't want to write anything further about Uncle Eustace's possessions. She would confess face to face. The silver pocket watch sat on the escritoire next to the blotter. A watch would be a useful addition to her disguise. She shook her head. No, she would not go out in Uncle's clothes anymore. But then again . . .

I am already looking forward to your return and hearing more about your travels. Maybe one day I too will have the opportunity to explore the continent.

Your loving daughter, as always, Hope

'It is time for luncheon, Hope,' Edna announced, after knocking gently on the door.

'Will I do?' Hope asked as she stood and smoothed down her dress. Edna was smiling sheepishly. 'What is it, Edna? Tell me, what's wrong?'

'It's your hair again. It's difficult to get it to look natural at this length.'

'I think you have been doing it very well. I doubt that anyone has noticed with the added hair pieces. Certainly Aunt Constance hasn't remarked on it. I'll sit here at the escritoire and you can see to it.' A picture of Beaumont flitted into her mind and she recollected his long, dark hair curling over his collar. Bringing herself back to the present, she noticed Edna glancing at the letter. 'I've written to my parents.'

'It's beautiful.'

Hope laughed. 'My writing is terrible. I have been in trouble many times for my untidiness.'

'But, my lady . . . '

'What is it, Edna, what's wrong?'

'It's beautiful to me because I can't write at all. Not one word, not even one letter of the alphabet.'

Hope was sorry she'd been thoughtless. There she was complaining about her untidy scrawl and Edna was unable to write at all.

'Would you like to learn? I could teach you while I'm here. I taught my maid at home. She *was* able to read and write a little, but now she can write letters and read simple stories.'

Edna looked wistful. 'It's more than I could wish for.'

'Then we'll start after luncheon if Aunt Constance is otherwise engaged.'

'I have already been asked by Her Grace to pack up His Grace's clothes for distribution.'

'Then that's what you must do and you will have a lesson another time. In another life I would have chosen to be a governess. Now, if my hair is acceptable I'll join my aunt. Thank you, Edna.'

Hope cantered down the stairs excited at the thought of helping Edna to read and write. Should she let her aunt know of her plan? Sometimes she could be difficult to fathom. Whilst Hope was sure Aunt Constance's intentions to help the poor and needy were well-founded, she thought perhaps it was on a more physical level such as giving them food and clothes. Also, she probably did not consider Edna to be needy as she was providing her with employment, a roof over her head and food for her stomach.

'May I ask you something?'

'Of course, my dear. What is on your mind?' Constance cut her pork and stabbed at it with her fork.

'At the wonderful dinner you hosted to welcome me to London, you . . . ' here Hope had to be careful not to mention Beaumont, ' . . . told Stevenson to distribute the leftover food to the underprivileged. Is that practice continuing?' She could feel the butler's cold stare like an icicle on the back of her neck, but she ignored him.

'Yes, it is. Not every day as we are quite a frugal household. And I am spending some time with Edna this afternoon sorting through your uncle's belongings in order that some of those may be given away. Eustace hated to see anyone cold or hungry. It upset him greatly.'

How very satisfactory to hear of the food distribution. Hope couldn't wait to impart the news to Beaumont. Perhaps she *could* risk mentioning his name. 'Does Beaumont know of your donations?' Constance raised her eyebrows. 'What I meant is, you and he conversed about it, I remember. Giving the leftover food to the poor.'

'That is so. And yes, Beaumont knows what happens here. We talked about it when he called to discuss the charity.'

'So Beaumont supports the fallen women? Oh, what I mean is the charity organisation, the Female Aid Society.'

'Hope.' Constance's tone was sharp. 'This is not appropriate conversation for luncheon. Perhaps this afternoon you should practise your pianoforte skills if you are to accompany Beaumont's slides.'

'It's strange he asked for me to play. He has a pianist who usually performs for him, doesn't he?' Hope compressed her lips quickly and firmly. What had she said?

'And how do you know that?' asked her aunt, putting another forkful of food into her mouth.

'It's what I suppose takes place. From what my parents have told me about the magic lantern shows.' Whatever had happened to her resolve to tell the truth whatever the consequences? The pudding was brought in. Although trifle was one of her favourite treats, she found her appetite had vanished.

★ ★ ★

The afternoon was interminably long and tedious. Hope didn't enjoy rehearsing her scales and wasn't very good at sight-reading music. She derived more pleasure from the covers of the scores than the printed notes inside. But Beaumont needed a proficient musician and she would do her best to provide him with one. Running her fingers up and down the keys, Hope's thoughts turned to teaching Edna how to read and write. That captivated her far more than the music she was trying to play. It would open up a completely new world for her maid, just as it had done for Ruth. Without realising it until she hit the final note, Hope had continued through a complete piece of music and was singing along with it.

It was at that point she decided that if she was not betrothed by the time she was thirty years old, she would ask Mama and Papa if she could be a governess. It was possible her parents might allow her if she explained it was her deepest desire, even though it was not the done thing for an earl's daughter. With that happy thought embedded in her mind, Hope raced up the stairs to her rooms. The rest of the afternoon would be spent with Uncle Eustace's books. Or she might sketch. The result wouldn't be as wonderful as her mother's art, of course, but she would try and improve that skill while she was in London.

Thoughts of her uncle had Hope scrabbling about in the cupboard for her masculine disguise. Uncle Eustace's clothes weren't there. Panic set in and her heart beat faster. Then she remembered the clothes hadn't been put away. Edna had come to the room, neatened her hair, and then Hope had gone down to luncheon. What had become of the clothes? Either Edna had tidied them away or she had returned them to their rightful place.

There were not many hiding places where Edna could have secreted them, but Hope made sure she looked everywhere she could think of. It was to no avail. As Aunt Constance was busy with the maid, Hope could not summon her and she spent a long time pacing the room wishing Edna would walk through the door.

In her mind dressing up as Richard was deeply connected to Beaumont and she couldn't bear missing any opportunity to see him. As Hope there might be one or two occasions when she could mix with him, but they would be few and far between. She did begin to wonder if she was suffering from a malady as Aunt Constance had suggested, but had no idea what it would be called or how treated. With no sign of Edna, Hope made her way yet again to Uncle Eustace's rooms. She thought that her aunt and the maid must have finished sorting Uncle Eustace's clothes by now. No one was in the room, just numerous piles of clothes. She was surprised when Stevenson entered along with one of the male servants.

'Lady Hope. I didn't know anyone was in here.'

'It's all right, Stevenson, I came to see if the task was completed or not.'

'As you can see my lady, these bundles of clothing are being taken now.' He gave a nod to the servant who proceeded to collect up some of the bundles and leave the room with them. 'That pile on the floor is the clothing

Her Grace thought was unsuitable to pass on.'

'Thank you, Stevenson.' As soon as the butler had left the room she dived into the bundle and grabbed items one after the other holding them up to see how fitting they were. In her view most were perfectly useable. Having sorted an outfit for Richard she surreptitiously left the room telling herself she was doing nothing wrong. Back in her room she hid the clothes at the bottom of her trunk. Then, to calm herself, she sat at the escritoire and continued with her journal.

I don't know what has come over me. I have behaved in a most unbecoming way. Scrabbling through clothes regarded as waste. Why did I do it? Because I wish to see Beaumont. If, after my attempt at playing the piano, he never wants to see me again I can at least view him from afar as Richard. What is it about him that makes my pulse quicken and cheeks pinken? I am ridiculous, I hardly know the man. But something, no everything, about him appeals — from his looks to his pursuits. When I next see Edna I will not tell her about the clothes I have taken. We will never speak of me dressing as a man again. But now I will dress as Richard and attempt to escape for a walk in one of the parks.

★ ★ ★

Hope felt comfortable in the clothes she had found and was pleased to have the watch tucked into the pocket of her waistcoat. It would ensure she was back in plenty of time and would not be missed. As her confidence increased she was able to enjoy all the sights and sounds of the street scenes around her. No longer did she hurry along, keeping her head down. She was certain no one would notice she was not what she seemed.

An enjoyable stroll in the weakening sunshine along the park's paths round the pond, gave her a feeling of peace. But on approaching Aunt Constance's house she was horrified to see Beaumont coming along the street in the opposite direction, clearly making his way to the front entrance. It was an unusual time to be making a social call uninvited. Her jauntiness ebbed and her legs turned to jelly. Looking down at her feet she tried not to falter and attempted to make her way past him without being seen. He stopped.

'Excuse me, it's Monsieur Richard, n'est pas?'

'Non,' she squeaked, before hurrying towards the side of the building and the back entrance. Once inside she leant against the door and vowed never again to risk going out in gentlemen's clothes. In her rooms she changed and stuffed the outfit in her trunk promising herself they would be returned to the pile later. Pacing the floor she wondered what had brought Beaumont here to her aunt's house again, and at such an unusual time to call. Had he realised she was not a man? Worse still, had he realised she was Hope and would he tell her aunt what he had seen? She hardly had time to recover from her confusion when there was a tap on the door. It was Edna bringing a request from Aunt Constance that Hope join her in the drawing room.

Twisting her hands and breathing shallowly, Hope asked, 'Why does she want me to join her, Edna?'

'Mr Beaumont is here. I overheard him say he wishes to discuss the magic lantern programme with you. Her Grace told me he wants to hear you play the accompaniment.'

'I can't possibly.'

'Your aunt will be displeased unless you are poorly. *Are* you ill?' Edna peered at her face.

Hope paused. Could she honestly say she was ill? No, not in a physical sense. What was she to do? Face the consequences of her actions. She straightened up. 'Very well, I will go down.' As she trudged down the stairs, she caught the timbre of Beaumont's voice and her body responded to it without any encouragement. She breathed deeply as she descended from the bottom stair and entered the drawing room.

'Ah, my dear, we have company. Beaumont would like to discuss your repertoire and listen to some of your pieces. We will have tea first in spite of it being rather late.' Aunt Constance gave Beaumont a withering look then nodded to the maid standing by the side table ready to serve the tea and delicacies.

Beaumont conferred a little bow to Hope and waited for her to be seated before he too sat. His eyes twinkled. 'Your aunt tells me you have been in your rooms all afternoon. Such a shame you weren't able to enjoy the fresh air. It is a beautiful day for a walk.'

'Humph. She can hardly go out alone, Beaumont, you know that.'

'It's a pity for the fairer sex. If she

were a man she could do as she pleases.'

He was making fun of her, Hope was sure. How dare he! She glared at Beaumont and to her horror he winked at her. As her cheeks grew warm, she wondered if her aunt had witnessed the bold gesture. She tried to look away, but Beaumont's eyes held hers.

As the maid approached, Hope let out the breath she was holding in. Never had tea been more welcome.

'When we have finished our refreshments, Hope, you must play for Beaumont,' said Constance.

The awkward moment had vanished. Beaumont continued with equable comments until finally he put down his cup and saucer and patted his mouth with a napkin.

Hope perched on the piano stool and fidgeted with a few pieces of sheet music. Beaumont stood next to her, her eyes level with his waistcoat buttons. 'You won't have seen my magic lantern shows, Hope, will you? Therefore you don't know the sort of music I need. Let me try and explain.'

Hope kept her eyes on the keys as he did so. Was she imagining the humour in his tone? He was teasing her again. It was on the tip of her tongue to ask in a whisper if he recognised her as being the young Frenchman, Richard, when he unexpectedly walked to the window and looked out. 'Play whatever you wish. We will make a list of the appropriate pieces when you have finished.'

'You will have to excuse me for a moment,' said Aunt Constance. 'Carry on with your playing, Hope. I shall return in a short while.' She put her hand to her head and walked from the room.

It didn't take long for Hope to go through her range of music and she floundered at times. With Beaumont in the same room, she found it hard to concentrate. At last she came to an end and brought down the piano lid with finality. She sat in silence waiting for

Beaumont to comment, but he, too, was silent. Unable to endure being in this situation any longer, she burst out, 'Why couldn't you have used your own pianist? She is far more accomplished than I am.'

Beaumont swung round and strode back towards Hope and the piano. 'And what do you know of her?'

'I . . . er, nothing, I . . . ' That was the second time she'd made the same mistake. What was the matter with her?

Beaumont crouched down on the carpet beside Hope and took her hand. 'We all have secrets, Hope. But I would like to think you could confide in me if you wished.'

With a nod of her head, she sprang up and distanced herself from him. The touch of his flesh, the rough texture of his jacket and the smell of him put her through an assortment of emotions that she couldn't comprehend. Her actions turned out to be well timed as Aunt Constance opened the door that very second and sailed into the room.

'Constance,' said Beaumont, upright again, 'your niece has hidden talents.' Hope refused to look at him. 'She has a delightful way of attacking the notes and I'm sure she will be an asset to the programme. Are you all right, Constance? You seem a little distressed.'

'I think the time spent in Eustace's rooms this afternoon tired me more than I thought it would. My head aches a little. I bathed my eyes, but I'd like to sit here a while. Why don't you escort Hope around the garden, Beaumont? She's still got a pallor about her and you remarked it was a shame for her to have been cooped up in her rooms.'

'An excellent suggestion,' smiled Beaumont. 'If Hope is agreeable.'

'I am aware it is not the done thing for my niece to be unchaperoned, but I can think of no alternative with this pain.' Constance clutched her head and closed her eyes. 'I'll get your maid to bring your shawl. It's fresh outside.'

Hope had no choice but to obey her aunt. Then she grasped what Edna's appearance could mean. Oh dear, it was too bad. Why hadn't she thought about it before and gone to fetch it herself? Edna came into the room and gasped when she caught sight of Beaumont. He came towards her and took the shawl she was holding. 'Thank you. I remember you, of course, but I don't know your name.'

'Really, Beaumont,' chided Constance, raising her head and frowning at him, 'you shouldn't be so free with the servants.'

He grinned at Edna. 'You remind me of someone's cousin.'

7

The fresh air revived Hope a little and she enjoyed the chance to walk in the garden. A short time ago she would have given anything for an opportunity such as this: to be with Beaumont strolling among the flowers and trees in her aunt's garden But she was in awe of him now as the unexplained secret hung between them. Although she felt unnerved by the situation, he probably did not. Nothing appeared to confound Beaumont. She stole a look at him. He ran his hand along the bark of a tree, tracing its intricate pattern with his fingers. For one flighty moment, she wished to change places with the tree bark. Then he spoke. 'Are you coming to the Female Aid Society benefit to please your aunt or are you interested in the work of its members?'

'I wish to know more of it. Mama

sometimes attended meetings, but I never have. I am willing to help anyone less fortunate than I am.' As she spoke, Hope felt enthusiasm coursing through her; the same feeling she'd had when she taught Ruth to read and write and when she contemplated doing the same with Edna. The thought of Edna reminded her of the conversation prior to this walk in the garden. She would not mention it, unless he brought it up. The discussion could continue about the disadvantaged.

'More than anything I should like to help people learn to read and write. Those two occupations give me such pleasure. I can't bear to think of anyone not knowing the joy of the written word or of letter writing or composing other works. My dreams are to teach and one day to write a book.' There, it was out in the open. He would surely laugh at her aspirations. When she looked at him, he was gazing at her with a serious expression.

Beaumont took her hand. 'Such soft

skin, Hope, and such sweet scent. Rose, isn't it?' This wasn't the response Hope had expected, but she couldn't deny it was agreeable. 'Your aims are admirable. I'm sure you will achieve them.'

The moment was broken by the hurried arrival of Edna. 'Hope, no I mean my lady,' Edna glanced at Beaumont, 'Her Grace told me to come into the garden and tell you it's time to go in now.'

'How is she, Edna?' Beaumont asked.

'She has a strong constitution, but I think she has been brought low by thoughts of His Grace.'

'He was a fine man.' Beaumont held out his arm for Hope to take. She hesitated and glanced at the windows of the house before linking her arm with his. They walked back along the path together, with Edna trailing behind. When they reached the entrance he patted her hand.

'I must leave you now. It has been most enjoyable spending time in your company. I trust you will be attending the Padstocks' ball this Saturday. Apparently it is one of the highlights of the season.'

'If Aunt Constance is fully recovered we will be there.'

'Good, I look forward to dancing with you.'

Hope wasn't sure if she was pleased or not as she watched him saunter away from them. Surely he should ask her if she wanted to dance with him, not assume that she would. But on the other hand she'd give almost anything to dance with him all evening, something she knew would definitely not be allowed.

⋆　⋆　⋆

Edna couldn't contain her anticipation on the day of the ball and skipped around Hope's room as she helped her get ready. 'This gold coloured ball gown is perfect for you, Hope. The line of it does justice to your trim waist and it's the very latest design. I sometimes see

Her Grace's magazines after she has discarded them and look at the pictures.'

Hope sat at the mirror while Edna styled her hair. 'I do think this single flower will look lovely, Hope. Its colour complements your dress perfectly.'

'What do you think about jewellery? I shouldn't wear too much. Do you think the bracelet Mama and Papa gave me before they left would do?'

'Perfectly. You're pretty as a picture.'

'But you still think I make a fine gentleman too?' They giggled and chatted until they were satisfied with Hope's appearance.

'Ah, good, I wondered when you would be ready. We should be leaving now.'

Hope had found her aunt looking rather wan sitting in the drawing room and gazing out of the window. 'Are you all right, Aunt? If you don't feel up to going I am quite happy to stay here with you.'

'We're going. James Henderson will

be there and I think he will be asking you for more dances than is acceptable!'

Hope wasn't sure if her aunt found that prospect good or bad.

'I have every wish that you and he will grow to like each other over the next few weeks and this ball is a chance for you to talk at least a little. I must remind you, however, that you should not dance too often with any one man. Maybe James will escort us to the refreshment room. Now send for our cloaks and we will set off.'

As they entered the Padstocks' mansion butterflies cavorted in Hope's stomach. She didn't want to dance with James Henderson, she wanted to dance with Beaumont and find out more about him. But she would have to be careful. There were always watchful eyes and word soon went round if anyone discredited themselves. The ballroom itself was alive with activity.

Her aunt nudged her. 'Look, he's there.' She pointed her fan in the direction of James. 'He'll be over soon to ask for the next dance, I'm sure of it.'

Hope wasn't concerned. James appeared to be looking in the direction of Isabella Padstock who was laughing coquettishly with yet another good-looking young man. As Hope glanced round the room she spotted Beaumont standing alone, deep in thought. She took a deep breath. He had to be the most handsome man in the room. His black dress-coat, waistcoat and white shirt set off his features to perfection. His beard was neatly trimmed and his hair dark and glossy. Just at that moment he looked up and their eyes met.

'Hope, Hope, dear, do pay attention. James is heading our way.'

The Honourable James Henderson duly stopped in front of then, bowing first respectfully to Constance and then to Hope. 'Will you favour me with your hand for the next dance?' he asked.

'With pleasure, sir,' Hope replied dutifully, handing over her card for him to inscribe his name.

As James stepped away Beaumont arrived.

'Good evening, Constance, Hope.' He inclined his head slightly to each of them in turn. 'Would you dance with me?'

Hope could barely speak. How she wished she could have his name on her card for all the dances. 'I regret I am engaged for the next dance, sir, but the one after that . . . well . . . ' She was lost for words.

'Hope! Here, Beaumont take her card and put your name down. She is inclined to giddiness. Not one of her best traits. But she is young, far younger than I and quite a few years younger than you.'

Beaumont raised his eyebrows. 'I believe Eustace was somewhat older than you, Constance. I am quite sure your love for each other was as strong as if you had been of similar ages.'

Love! How had love come into the conversation? Hope looked from her aunt to Beaumont and back to her aunt again.

'Indeed Beaumont. This is quite the most inappropriate conversation for the occasion. Thankfully here comes James.'

James led Hope onto the dance floor and the quadrille began. Hope liked dancing and was soon enjoying herself, but was aware of Beaumont standing watching her, his eyes on her every move. It was quite disconcerting. When the dance ended James led her back to the seat next to her aunt, thanked her, bowed politely and left. Beaumont was soon back, a grin on his face. 'My turn I believe.'

'Really Beaumont, your manners are . . .'

'I apologise, but this young lady dances like an angel and I can't wait to whisk her round the ballroom.'

'Be warned. I will be watching, along with all the other mothers and aunts in the room.' Hope couldn't be sure, but there seemed to be a twinkle in her aunt's eye.

All other thoughts soon disappeared from Hope's mind as Beaumont's arm encircled her waist and she felt the warmth of his hand through the light material of her gown. When their hands met, she feared she'd have the vapours and she had to hang on tightly to him. Secretly, she was pleased to have the excuse to do so. Not that he was a stabilising influence on her at all. The jaunty polka music had its effect and Beaumont skilfully whisked her across the ballroom; it was as if they were the only two in the whole room. Risking a glance at him as they twirled around, Hope's eyes met his and he tightened his hold on her, pulling her closer to him. If only this could go on forever. But then the music stopped and partners separated.

Beaumont escorted Hope to Aunt Constance who was in conversation with Isabella Padstock. Could it be possible that Beaumont would ask her for another dance, pondered Hope. She willed him to read her mind. He leant towards her and she was sure he had. 'Thank you, Hope. You're a splendid dancer as I said. I would ask you for the next dance, but I am promised to another.'

Hope wondered if he would be dancing with Isabella. Lady Padstock wouldn't be pleased, she reflected. But after acknowledging Isabella, Beaumont extended his hand towards her aunt. 'Our dance I think, Constance. I'm looking forward to it. The young people quite tire me.' He inclined his head to Hope and winked. As Beaumont led Constance away, Hope heard him saying, 'I'm pleased you feel able to take a stage out of mourning. What a very pretty sash that is.'

To Hope's surprise, she saw that her aunt was a more than capable dancer. She watched as Beaumont expertly guided his partner around to the waltz music.

'I see you danced with James.' Isabella's voice took Hope by surprise; she'd forgotten she was there.

'Yes,' she said, dragging her eyes from the dance floor. 'He's a competent partner.' It was all she could think of to say about him.

'He's divine,' breathed Isabella. 'He's written his name in for the maximum number of allowed dances.'

Hope was relieved that Isabella and The Honourable James Henderson were getting on well together. 'It's a wonderful evening, Isabella. I'm especially pleased to see Aunt Constance enjoying herself as much as she is.'

A queue of young gentlemen approached the two women and asked for their dance cards. Hope's was filling rapidly and she wanted there to be room for Beaumont's name. How many dances were they allowed together? She couldn't remember, but she knew her aunt would and she would also check to make sure etiquette prevailed.

Suddenly there was a commotion on the dance floor and Hope looked up to see Beaumont with his arm around

Aunt Constance. James was on the other side as they half-carried her to the edge of the ballroom and sat her gently into a chair. Lady Padstock attended immediately and directed the dancing to continue.

A screen was placed strategically to provide her with privacy and Constance put a hand to her head. 'Aunt,' whispered Hope, 'how can I help? Has your headache returned?' Constance nodded and looked tearful.

'Drink this,' directed Beaumont, holding out a glass of brandy. 'I think you exerted yourself too much.'

He treated the patient with such kindness Hope was near tears. Much as she hated to admit it, she realised her aunt should be taken home without delay. When she voiced her opinion, both Constance and Beaumont agreed. 'I'll get your carriage brought round to the closest entrance,' said Beaumont.

'Poor Constance,' whispered Lady Padstock. 'It was a great pleasure for us that you should come this evening with your dear niece. But now you must return home and rest.'

Beaumont and Hope helped Constance to the carriage. Beaumont tucked a rug around her. 'I wish you a restful night, Constance.' Holding out his hand to aid Hope into the carriage, her heart fluttered as he drew nearer and she was sure he was about to kiss her. If she acted instinctively, she would move forward and instigate an embrace; if she followed the line of propriety, she'd back away that instant. In the event, she did neither. Beaumont raised her hand to his lips and caressed it before letting go. Hope ducked into the carriage, sure her hammering heartbeat must be audible.

By the time they arrived at the house, Constance appeared a little brighter, but still exhausted.

With Aunt Constance safely indoors, Hope left her to the ministrations of the servants. Perhaps the doctor should be called in the morning. As Hope readied herself for bed, she was lost in a dream of what might have been if her dance card had been filled with Beaumont's name and, more excitingly, if she and he had been alone outside the Padstocks' mansion with the carriage as their refuge.

8

When Edna entered the room the following morning, Hope's first thoughts were of her aunt. 'How is Aunt Constance today, Edna?'

'She was sitting up in bed and drinking tea. That would seem a good sign.'

Hope nodded her head. 'I'm sure you're right. Poor Aunt. If she'd stayed at home last evening she could have had the rest she sorely needs. I feel certain she made a special effort on my behalf.'

Edna's eyes lit up. 'Was it a wonderful evening? Apart from Her Grace being took poorly, I mean.'

'It was most enjoyable. I managed to have two dances; one with James Henderson and the other with Beaumont.'

'Hope, I do envy you. The Honourable James is very attractive, even if he isn't very exciting.'

'And what about Beaumont? Don't you find him striking?'

'For an older man, certainly he is.' Edna darted around the room tidying Hope's garments which she'd strewn about the previous night. 'I'm sorry I wasn't available to put your clothes away. I did tap on the door after we'd settled your aunt, but there was no reply.'

'That's quite all right, Edna. Aunt Constance must come first. And I should have been more careful with my things. The dress is very elegant, isn't it?' Hope stretched and rolled out of bed. 'Now I must get ready for breakfast.'

* * *

Just as she was swallowing her last mouthful of devilled kidneys and toast, she was informed a visitor had arrived to enquire after Her Grace. It must be Lady Padstock, surmised Hope. She rose from the table and went to the drawing room. To her shame, she hadn't seen her aunt since the previous evening.

When Hope caught sight of the visitor she nearly fainted. It was Beaumont, the last person she expected to see so early in the morning. He came towards her. 'Hope, I came to ask how Constance is. I was worried about her yesterday and wanted to reassure myself that she isn't any worse.'

'I'm afraid I haven't visited her yet. I understand she is still in bed and has managed to sip some tea. I thought it best that she have some time to herself to recover. If you wished to see her then I'm sorry your journey here has been wasted.'

'On the contrary, I would say my journey has been rewarded already.' Beaumont's eyes crinkled at the corners as he smiled down at her.

'I shall inform my aunt that you were here and I will pass on your best regards for her health.'

'Please don't dismiss me now,' pleaded Beaumont. 'I have things I wish to discuss with you, Hope.'

She risked a look at Stevenson who was hovering by the door as if standing guard. She beckoned Beaumont to the far corner of the room, wanting to be out of earshot of the butler. 'How may I be of assistance?' she enquired politely, trying to keep the tone of her voice calm, even though her body was trembling at his very nearness. She could smell his fresh manly scent and compared it favourably to the tobacco reek of James Henderson.

'The magic lantern show for the charity event is on my mind,' began Beaumont. 'Often I narrate the stories, but you will be playing the piano for some of them and I should like the audience to be able to know some of the underlying metaphors. Would you assist me in writing a little about them? I remember you confided in me your aims were to teach and write a book. These two ambitions of yours qualify you perfectly for the post. What do you say?'

The mention of writing ensnared her immediately. 'Do you usually provide written matter for your audiences?' asked Hope. On her visit with Edna she hadn't been aware of anything like that being available. She wanted to know everything about Beaumont and his shows.

'Sometimes I do, but they are not always well received. 'I've no idea why.' Beaumont's good looks were momentarily marred as a frown creased his forehead. 'I've tried to make the information engaging, but . . . ' His voice tailed away.

'Have you tried making it *too* fascinating, I wonder?' ventured Hope. 'I ask because when I was teaching my maid, Ruth, to read and write I found I was trying too hard and complicating things for her unnecessarily. She was unable to follow the words I was choosing.'

'You see, Hope, you're an inspiration.

I think you're correct. We need something far simpler. I've a feeling a good proportion of the audience are unable to read well or even at all. Probably not at the Female Aid Society performance, but at the shows held at fairs and music halls. There's more to helping the underprivileged than handing out food parcels, although they are essential of course.'

Beaumont's vibrant face delighted Hope. She recognised the enthusiasm they shared.

'Aunt Constance has continued to donate leftover food since your visit here when you broached the subject, and the clothes belonging to Uncle Eustace which she tired herself so dreadfully in sorting, they are to be given away also. Indeed, I believe they already have been. Most of them.' Hope felt her cheeks grow warm as she added the last sentence.

'I am pleased. But I think it is down to you being so caring, Hope. I've never met a woman like you. Most of the ladies I come across think only of themselves and their looks. You, on the other hand, are a compassionate person as well as a beautiful and intelligent one.'

Luckily Beaumont had lowered his voice and Hope wished with all her might that Stevenson hadn't overheard their conversation. She had never had so many compliments heaped upon her and thought she would collapse under the weight of them. In order to maintain her equilibrium she murmured, 'Shall we return to the question in hand, Beaumont? Do you think it would be an improvement if I were to sketch replicas of your slides and put one or two apposite words underneath, simple ones which could possibly be understood. Then the audience might take them away and study them at their leisure. That's what Ruth did and that's what I want to do with Edna.'

'You also have extreme vision and patience. The latter is something I am aware I am sadly lacking.'

In the pause which followed Stevenson coughed discreetly.

'I think it is time I went, but I will call soon with a selection of slides for you to sketch. I'm looking forward to working with you.' He glanced at Stevenson. 'But only if your aunt agrees to our collaboration.'

'I'm sure she will. She has a very good heart. Do you suppose you could also teach me how to paint the slides? I would like to create my own story.'

Beaumont nodded thoughtfully. 'Of course. Au revoir, Hope.' He smiled, made a little bow, took her hand and kissed it before leaving the room.

Hope caught her breath and flung herself into the nearest chair. Her feelings were in turmoil. She would go to her rooms and write her journal which always had a soothing effect.

Beaumont, Beaumont, Beaumont. How he affects me. When we danced at the ball it felt as though we belonged in each other's arms. Given the chance to dance with him all night, I would have done, whatever anyone thought of me. And now, if Aunt agrees, I will be spending time with him as we prepare for the magic lantern show. Aunt does not approve of him still. She made a comment about his age, yet he isn't so very much older than me, maybe ten years. Au revoir is a common enough phrase, but I wonder why Beaumont chose to say it. Am I reading too much into things?

⋆   ⋆   ⋆

'My lady, Hope, Lady Isabella is here to see you.'

'What does she want? Have you any idea?' Hope was puzzled as she thought Isabella would much have preferred to be shopping or titivating to calling on her.

'I don't know. She is in the drawing room.' Edna stood by the door as if expecting Hope to rush down to greet Isabella.

'Very well.' Hope closed her journal and went to find out the reason for Isabella's visit.

As she entered the drawing room Isabella turned from the window.

'I wanted to ask after the Duchess. How is she?'

Hope should have known Isabella hadn't called to see her, but she acknowledged it was thoughtful of her to ask after Aunt Constance.

'Feeling a little better, thank you. Beaumont came to ask after her.' Hope could feel her cheeks flushing. Even as she said his name, his face materialised before her and she had to blink the image away.

'Beaumont? I think he has grown fond of you. Love is wonderful, don't you think? I couldn't sleep at all after the ball and having spent time with James. So this morning I decided to get up early and then I had a sudden desire to call and see you to talk about the events of last night. I'm afraid I danced with James too many times, almost every dance, and Mama is rather cross with me. He didn't write them all on my card. Is what I did very wrong?'

Hope giggled. 'No, I do not think so at all, but I am rather surprised you did not adhere to the etiquette. I think you should go and be with your mama and restore yourself to her good graces.'

★ ★ ★

Hope had a lot to write.

Isabella has astounded me. I would never have thought she would behave in such a way. I thought the Padstock girls were impeccably brought up and knew the etiquette of every occasion. Will James love her more for her daring acts? Love has a strange way of transcending things. I am sure it is true that one can feel love for someone older or younger and from a different background.

While I wait for Beaumont to return, and I confess I am counting the minutes, I will concentrate on teaching

Edna to read. She has shown she has an interest in fashion so I will draw some pictures and cut some from magazines and write simple words to go with them. Where will I take her lesson? Here in my rooms or below stairs? If the latter what will Stevenson think?

I have had another idea. If I paint some slides to go with a story then maybe Beaumont would arrange for the servants to have their own private magic lantern show. Would that be allowed or will Stevenson put his foot down?

Hope closed her journal and paced across the room. Now she'd written about the classes she was going to give, she wanted to get started. On a shelf there were some magazines her aunt had let her have. Turning their pages, she found just the things she was looking for: pictures of pretty dresses, accessories and trifles which she felt sure Edna would love. She would cut them out and arrange them before deciding what words were appropriate to write alongside them. At last her discarded embroidery was to come in useful. Quickly she picked up the scissors intended to cut the silks and applied them to the paper. With such a small tool it was painstakingly slow, but Hope didn't mind. As she performed the task, her thoughts ran ahead to the completed assignment. This wasn't just for Edna and possibly the other servants, it was for Beaumont also. The more she knew about him, the more he pleased her. He had said he wasn't patient, but Hope had witnessed him tending her aunt and a more considerate person she could not wish to know. If only her aunt thought more of him. Then she corrected herself; she was sure her aunt regarded him with esteem. Indeed, she'd as much as admitted that, but she did not view him as a proper suitor for Hope. But then again, perhaps Beaumont didn't harbour such notions himself. Perhaps he had no wish to court her at all and simply wanted her help. Well, for now, that would suffice.

As Hope would have to ask Edna where she could obtain glue to stick the pictures to the paper, she put them to one side and picked up a pencil to sketch a copy of the fan she'd presented to her maid when they'd been to the dressmaker's shop. She was pleased with the drawing and underneath she wrote the letters: FAN. Then she turned her attention to the next idea she had for a picture. Before she knew it, the time had passed and Edna was knocking at her door.

'Hope, it's time to change and go to luncheon. Her Grace has made an effort to be in the dining room.'

Putting on her green and pink dress, Hope let Edna brush and pin her hair. She saw her looking at the sketches she'd made. 'What do you think of those, Edna?'

'They're pretty. Did you do them? You're very clever. I like to draw, but I'm not much good.' She left her task to inspect the picture of the fan. 'That must say fan I suppose. Is that right?'

Hope clapped her hands. 'You see, you are clever, Edna. That's exactly what it says. You can read.'

Edna's cheeks went bright red. 'I can read my name, that's all. But I cannot form the letters.'

'You can read fan as well now. What a quick pupil you are.' The large smile on Edna's face warmed Hope's heart.

*   *   *

Hope was delighted to see her aunt dressed and almost looking her normal self. 'How are you feeling?' she asked as she put an arm gently around the older woman's shoulders and kissed her soft cheek.

'Much better, thank you.' She patted Hope's hand. 'I am sorry we had to cut short our visit to the ball. It was proving an enjoyable night.'

Oh, much more than merely enjoyable, thought Hope. 'It was a wonderful evening even if it was brief. There will be other balls,' she said. She took her seat opposite her aunt. She wasn't hungry, but knew she had to make a pretence. Whatever was the matter with her? Usually she could eat anything and everything.

She wondered what Aunt Constance was going to eat, as a full meal would be too much of an onslaught to her digestion after being indisposed. 'What are you having?' she enquired.

'Beef tea and toast. And the cook sent word she's boiled an arrowroot pudding for me.' To Hope's amusement, her aunt gave a little shudder and the vestige of a smile.

'How simply delicious,' chuckled Hope, picking up her knife and fork to tackle the plate of boiled beef and vegetables which was put before her. The least she could do was be thankful she didn't have the same menu as Aunt Constance.

It had been a very busy morning for Hope and, as she ate, she tried to put the events in order in her mind. She started with the most important. 'Beaumont called to ask after you early this morning. He wishes you good health.'

Her aunt nodded. 'He's proving to be a considerate acquaintance. The more I see of him, the more I understand why Eustace thought well of him. It does not, however, excuse his outspokenness.' She frowned as she sipped her beef tea.

Hope decided to omit the details of Isabella's visit and the tutorials she was proposing to hold for literacy. But her aunt was entitled to a bit more news. 'Beaumont asked me to assist him with the writing of a few sentences to explain the stories he shows from his magic lantern.'

'Oh? Why can't he do that himself? Don't let him, or anyone else, take advantage of you, my dear.'

Hope blushed at the thought . . .

★   ★   ★

After luncheon, Hope sought out Edna. 'We'll hold the lesson in my room.'

'It could be a little awkward. I told two of my friends in the kitchen you are going to teach me to read and they want to learn too. Would it be possible?'

'I'll be delighted to teach your friends. But you are right, it would not do for them to come to my room. Is there somewhere else we can go to begin our lessons?'

Edna nodded and replied, 'We could . . . no, that's not a good idea.'

'Please tell me, Edna,' encouraged Hope.

'Well, the cook is going out this afternoon. I know it's not proper, but you could come to the servants' hall.'

'That *is* a good idea.' Although the notion had crossed her mind she wanted Edna to take the credit.

Hope was sure she was not complying with the rules of etiquette, but if there was no one around to chastise her she would continue as she thought fit.

After all, she was only trying to improve literacy; she was committing no sin.

They arranged to meet in a short while. Hope collected all the things she thought she would need and stealthily made her way down the back stairs. It was a shame the floor coverings were so worn here, any of the servants could easily lose their footings and trip. She would mention it to her aunt who must surely be unaware of these things. But how could she do that without implicating herself? At that moment, Hope felt she was being sucked into another thread of deception she had no right to be in, but she dismissed it from her mind for the time being. No one would know; no one would tell her aunt of her inappropriate visits below stairs.

On reaching her destination, she gasped in shock. Standing, as if awaiting her, was Stevenson. He scowled at her and almost spat out the words, 'How may I be of assistance, Lady Hope?'

9

Hope put on her most authoritative voice. 'It's quite all right, Stevenson, please carry on.'

'Yes, Lady Hope.' Stevenson turned and walked back to the butler's pantry.

Hope tried to calm herself before entering the servants' hall where Edna and the two other young maids were seated. As soon as Hope walked in they stood.

'This won't do,' Hope told them. 'We must forget all the formalities. You mustn't think of me as Lady Hope. I am simply here to teach you to read. Let's start by looking at these pictures.' She spread the papers on the table and they all sat down and started talking.

It seemed like just a minute before Stevenson was standing in the doorway, looking over at them. 'Lady Hope, the cook and the housekeeper have returned.'

Edna hurriedly gathered together the papers and Hope scurried to the back stairs clutching them, allowing herself to breathe deeply and wonder at Stevenson's change of heart.

Now she would write to Ruth and tell her all about her latest venture. But she must remember to use simple words.

Dear Ruth,

How are you? And your family?

I am very happy as I am teaching some of the servants to read. I use pictures, as I did with you.

I have so much to tell you about my stay in London.

Have you read any of the books you took with you? I would very much like to hear from you with your news.

Your friend,
Hope

She leant back in the chair and closed her eyes. It was only a few days before the twenty-first when she would be playing the piano at the magic lantern show. She had very little time to prepare the illustrations. Beaumont must call soon surely. For now she would lie on the bed and dream of their next meeting.

She was woken by a tap on the door. Edna entered carrying a parcel.

'Her Grace told me to bring this to you. Mr Beaumont called and wished to see you, but Her Grace said it was quite unnecessary and she would have the parcel sent up to you. She also said there was no need for him to collect your drawings as she would have them sent to his house.'

'Oh.' Hope felt disappointed.

'And there is also this.' Edna handed her a white envelope. 'I was with Her Grace when Mr Beaumont called and he slipped this into my hand. I think it says Hope on the envelope. I remember from when you showed us how you write your name in our lesson.'

Hope's feelings soared. 'Thank you,

Edna, you may go now. And well remembered. You are right, it does say my name.' She tore the envelope open with trembling fingers.

My dearest Hope,

I have written this letter with the thought that I may not be able to speak to you alone. I may have led you to believe I have feelings for you as a woman. Since meeting you I have not felt quite myself. However I do not want to mislead you. I have never seen my future as a married man and I will soon be going back to my home town to oversee our mill. In spite of having a manager who knows the trade as well as I do, I still need to attend to certain aspects of the business. Maybe it is for the best, but meantime I would be honoured if you would agree to spend some time with me so that we may store memories to look back on.

Ever yours,
Beaumont

Whatever did he mean? Hope read the letter several times before tossing it on the table. One moment it sounded as though he cared for her and the next he was leaving London. She would speak to him at the magic lantern show and find out exactly what he was trying to say. She undid the knot on the parcel and carefully unwrapped the slides. Several immediately appealed and she quickly found her sketch book and started the work knowing that she would please Beaumont, if not the audience.

★   ★   ★

Hope was in a state of consternation as the time drew near to attend the magic lantern show. She was still deeply puzzled by Beaumont's letter, and the thought of being in his company with unresolved matters standing between them was more than she could countenance.

Aunt Constance was feeling somewhat better and was going with her. Hope tried not to concentrate too much on her appearance, but hoped Beaumont would appreciate the plain style of dress she had chosen for the event.

As they entered the hall Hope immediately saw Beaumont and felt a mixture of emotions. Her blood heated as she thought of the night of the ball. In Beaumont's arms, she had felt she belonged to him and wished the feelings were mutual, but the letter he'd sent to her appeared to refute that. If he really cared for her he would stay in London or at least indicate his intention of returning to her. Her throat constricted with unshed tears which would not do at all. The evening ahead demanded her full attention. She led her aunt to a chair near the front.

'I think you will see well here, Aunt.'

'Thank you, my dear. I hope the music will give everyone a great deal of pleasure. Ah, what's this?' A young man handed her a sheet of paper. 'It's your work. Hope. And very professional it is too. Yes, yes, quite perfect. Oh, my dear, I do wish Eustace was here. He would be proud of you.'

Hope felt a breath on the back of her neck and she immediately knew Beaumont was behind her. 'Would you like to take your place and play the introductory piece we chose?'

Despite her misgivings as to her competence at playing the piano, Hope performed well. In fact, she enjoyed matching the tune to the pictures on the screen. She was also happy to see her aunt and several of the audience referring to her illustrated sheet throughout the performance. Pride goes before a fall, as the good book says, thought Hope when she brought her fingers down on two wrong notes. The jarring chord sounded atrocious, but she didn't dare risk a look at either Beaumont or the audience in case she made more mistakes. The story came to an end and the applause was long and loud.

One of the committee ladies from the Female Aid Society announced there would be refreshments in a side room. Hope should accompany her aunt, but first she had to prepare the sheet music for the pieces after the interval. As she scrabbled through the pages, there was a movement beside her. Beaumont, she knew.

'Outstanding,' he said, the glimmer of a smile on his face.

'Apart from the incorrect chord,' grimaced Hope.

'It came at the appropriate moment. It enhanced the stormy scene. Very well placed indeed. Don't tell me it was an accident.' His dark eyes bore into hers and she was at a momentary loss for words.

She laughed and confessed, 'It was definitely an accident.'

'Then you should make them more often. Have there been any other mistakes you wish to admit to?'

He was surely teasing her. Hope

shook her head thoroughly. She had no wish whatsoever to admit to anything! 'I must accompany Aunt Constance. Please excuse me.' She stood up and made to pass him, but he positioned himself in front of her and she found herself with barely an inch between them. It made her heart flutter.

'Constance has already gone through to the refreshment room. She has many friends here and it is an informal occasion.' Beaumont spoke lightly, but he didn't move. 'Hope, I must talk to you. I didn't think we'd have an opportunity, but one has just presented itself. Please may we make the most of it?'

'I shouldn't be with you.' Hope looked around the room, but no one was taking the least bit of notice of them. Perhaps it would be all right for them to converse. There were things that needed to be said, although she wasn't sure what.

'I sent you a letter . . . ' began Beaumont looking and sounding uncharacteristically unsure of himself.

Regardless of her own disappointment, Hope felt sorry for him. Hesitancy didn't suit him. 'You did,' she put in. Now was not a time to be cautious; there might never be another opportunity to air the questions she had. 'I will inform you that I found your company at the ball very pleasing. You are a fine partner.' She gulped as she realised the implication of the word she'd chosen. 'You dance well,' she amended. 'I, too, felt we shared an affinity, but it seems it is not very strong on your part if you are to take yourself away before . . . ' Hope was mortified. Whatever was possessing her to reveal her emotions like this? It was a most improper way to behave.

Her resolutions of asking Beaumont why he felt they couldn't be together when he had confided some feelings for her vanished. At the moment her voice would not come out without a wobble. And what did he mean about storing memories for the future? According to him, it didn't appear as if they had one, at least not together. Perhaps it would have been better if he hadn't sent the letter at all.

She felt his hand take hers, but could not pull away.

'Hope, I am not worthy of you and it is better if I put distance between us.' He seemed on the verge of adding something else, but a member of the charity came to him and he let go of her hand, excusing himself from her.

Feeling distraught and dissatisfied, Hope trailed towards the refreshments, thinking a cup of tea would revive her. She didn't understand what Beaumont meant. How could he be unworthy? He was one of the most worthy people she knew.

She was greeted enthusiastically as she made her way to the table upon which the food and drink were laid out.

'Such a wonderful performance. And the addition of the drawings and captions make the sheets a perfect souvenir of the occasion.' Several of the audience echoed the sentiments and Hope began to feel restored. All she had to do was get through the rest of the show and then she could escape home with Aunt Constance. She edged nearer to her and was welcomed into the friendly coterie. Immersed as she was in the subject of the good works of the charity, she didn't notice Beaumont until she heard his voice.

'Constance,' he said, much to the apparent consternation of the others present, 'I need to have a word with your charming niece. There's something she needs to be aware of during the next part of the programme. Will you excuse her, please?'

Aunt Constance inclined her head. 'There is a little time remaining before the performance resumes.'

Beaumont offered Hope his arm and then led her to the almost-deserted hall. 'If I could make you understand how I feel, I am sure you would forgive me.' He looked so lost, Hope wanted to put an arm about him and comfort him. 'I have been witness to much poverty and its attendant ills: disease, hunger, homelessness, degradation.' Beaumont shook his head and his eyes moistened. 'Although I am not as privileged as some here today, I consider myself fortunate that I have a roof over my head and food on my table. I admire you greatly and one day you will be married to someone worthy of you. Please believe me when I say it gives me no pleasure to distance myself from you. I am growing fonder of you each day.'

At his words, Hope wanted to plant a loving kiss on his cheek and reassure him the feelings were reciprocated. But she was aware her aunt was a short distance away. She must not bring disgrace to the family, even if she had already acted dreadfully at times.

A member of the audience approached them. 'A remarkable show. Such a lot for the two of you to execute. If you need an assistant, don't hesitate to ask. I'd be honoured and willing to help.'

Beaumont looked his old self and his eyes twinkled as he replied, 'That is most kind. I did have the offer of help, but I was badly let down by the young gentleman in question.' Hope turned her back unwilling to witness the expression on Beaumont's face.

Alone again, Beaumont whispered. 'I understand why Richard couldn't be here today. I'm glad you're here instead of him.'

'Whatever do you mean?' Hope knew the cat was out of the bag. She sagged against a chair. 'Yes, you're right in your supposition. But I've put an end to it. It was meant for fun.'

The loud roar of laughter that Beaumont let out startled Hope. 'You're unique, Hope. Do you know that?'

'Aren't we all, Beaumont?' Hope's lips tilted upwards.

The audience was returning. 'If Richard had one last wish, what would it be?' Beaumont's tone was amused, but now his eyes were serious.

Without having to think about it, Hope replied, 'To visit a gentlemen's club.'

Beaumont nodded. 'Consider it arranged. Come to the fair on Thursday before luncheon and we will dine out.'

'The two of us?' If Beaumont were found out Hope was certain he would be expelled from the club. Quickly she voiced her thought.

'I don't care if I *am* drummed out,' shrugged Beaumont. 'It would be worth it.'

Their eyes met and this time it was Beaumont who broke the contact.

Hope was on the verge of yet another exploit. Despite it being unseemly, it would be exciting and a wonderful experience. Also, it would give her time alone with Beaumont. Perhaps then she would find out the truth behind his puzzling letter.

10

My Dearest Beaumont,

Thursday feels such a very long time away, I can scarcely contain myself. Aunt Constance has admonished me several times for being fidgety and not listening to her. I hope she doesn't suspect anything. I am worried that I will not be able to escape at the appropriate hour and you will be left waiting and think I have changed my mind about meeting you. That I would never do.

In my head I go over the times we have been close. When you helped me into the carriage after the ball and I thought you would kiss me — there I've said it. When you held my hand at the magic lantern show. If only you knew how your look, your touch, your words affect me. And yet you are an enigma. Your lack of a title, the way you seem entranced by me one minute and the next are heading for the wilds of the north, the fact that you regard yourself as unworthy. I am mystified.

I never imagined I would feel like this. I have been introduced to many gentlemen, but never have I felt the sensations I feel when I see you or even think about you.

Enough for now.

Your loving Hope

Hope read the letter and tore it into little pieces. She had never intended to send it to Beaumont; she simply wanted to put her feelings on paper to see if she could make sense of them. It hadn't helped.

She decided to occupy her mind with another lesson for Edna and her friends. When it had been arranged and she entered the servants' hall, Stevenson was talking to the cook, who acknowledged her presence and left the room.

'Lady Hope, I wonder if I could have a word.' He looked unusually uncomfortable.

Hope's heart plummeted. Her plans to help the young girls in service here was going to be thwarted. 'Of, course, Stevenson.'

'I doubt you know much about me, there is no need for you to do so. When I started in service as the hallboy, the butler at the house took me under his wing. He taught me to write. He also taught me everything I needed to know to progress my career. I have no idea why.'

'He saw your potential, Stevenson.'

Stevenson looked flustered. 'Possibly. Without his help I would not be in the position of butler here.' Hope could almost see his chest puffing out. He was very proud of his status and rightly so she thought. 'In view of my experience I would be prepared to overlook your visits to the servants' hall, but you are putting us all in an untenable position which might result in us losing our jobs.

You must tell Her Grace, or I will have to do so myself.'

'Quite right, Stevenson and thank you for your understanding. I will tell Aunt Constance at dinner this evening.' In spite of trying to sound confident Hope could already feel her knees trembling at the thought of telling her aunt about her visits below stairs. She attempted to concentrate on the lesson and not dwell on the forthcoming confrontation.

The way the servants applied themselves to their lesson delighted Hope. It was very rewarding to put pictures before the young women and ask them to choose the correct word to place beside them. She'd expanded the pictures from fashion to food and animals. The latter she'd drawn herself and had enjoyed doing so. There was a stray cat which she often saw from her window, and in the street outside the morning room she caught sight of mangy dogs roaming around.

When the lesson ended, she asked if

there were any pictures they'd like for next time. As soon as she'd asked the question, she was aware that there might not be a next time. Her insides knotted as she remembered she had to broach the subject with her aunt. While Aunt Constance had softened considerably since Hope's arrival, this particular situation could only have one outcome she feared. She would be instructed to give up her teaching.

At dinner she could feel Stevenson's eyes on her. She looked at him and received an encouraging if almost imperceptible nod.

'Aunt, I have a confession. I have done something improper, but I think it was for the best of reasons. You must judge for yourself.'

'Well, my dear, you clearly didn't follow Isabella's example and partner the same man for almost every dance. Perhaps given the opportunity you would have. Are you running away with a soldier? That can't be it because you say you have already committed the improper act. It is clear it is of little significance or you would be wringing your hands and weeping. Come along, dear, tell me, nothing much shocks me anymore.'

After Hope had explained, Constance smiled then raising her voice said, 'And where were you, Stevenson, when these lessons were taking place below stairs?'

'I was there, Your Grace. I saw what was going on and allowed it to continue,' Stevenson conceded.

'Really? Whatever next?'

'It wasn't anything to do with Stevenson, Aunt.' Hope didn't want anyone else to take the blame for her misdemeanour.

'No, it was all to do with Beaumont, wasn't it? Clearly this is his influence at work.' Constance indicated for the empty plates to be taken away.

'Not really. I taught my maid at home to read. We exchange letters. Mama thought it was a good idea and encouraged me.' Hope wasn't sure whether involving her mother was the best thing.

'I am too weary to argue. You are a good woman, as is your mother in her unique way, and I am quite sure there is no reason for you not to go below stairs for this purpose. However, let us make sure Lady Padstock does not hear about this or we will be the talk of the neighbourhood for a very long time. Although I don't think Lady Padstock will be finding fault with others for the time being. Now, Stevenson, what do we have for pudding?'

Later Hope wrote in her journal with enthusiasm.

I am unable to believe I am allowed to continue with the lessons. Aunt Constance is hard to fathom. Sometimes everything has to be proper and sometimes we can do as we please and forget the proprieties. I am very happy, but wonder if I should still meet Beaumont dressed as Richard. Aunt Constance has been very good to me and I think she would collapse if she found out I was going into public dressed as a man . . . and to a gentlemen's club. It is outrageous. Even I admit that. My heart pounds when I think about it. It is hard to imagine how I will feel when the time comes.

*   *   *

Fortune favoured Hope. On Thursday her aunt sent a message that she would be spending the morning in her room. She insisted she was quite well, just a little tired. She would meet Hope for afternoon tea and begged Hope's forgiveness for her lack of attention.

Hope almost danced around the room, but feelings of guilt at her deception and anxiety over her aunt's constitution, prevented her from much jubilation. As she pulled the clothes from the trunk she realised they were not suitable for attending a gentlemen's club. Why hadn't she thought of that before? These clothes were the ones which were to be discarded as rags. Then she remembered the other clothing she had worn which had disappeared from her room.

She rang for her maid. 'Edna, where are the clothes which I originally took from Uncle Eustace's room? Do you know?'

'They are under my mattress. I didn't know where to hide them so pushed them under there. No one will look. They are quite safe until you tell me what I should do with them.'

'I would like to see them. Please bring them here and then I would like to be left alone until it is time for tea.'

'Shall I bring you some luncheon?'

'No, thank you. I am bursting out of my new dresses so will try to eat a little less for a few days. Please fetch the clothes now.'

Moments later Hope studied her reflection. Any doubts she had were dispelled when she thought of Beaumont. With him by her side, she could do anything.

* ★ ★

At the appointed hour, Hope left the house quietly and furtively. She had to remain positive that no one would see her and wonder who the unknown gentleman leaving Her Grace's house was. After she'd gone a little way, she let out the breath she was holding and slowed down her pace. There was only a short distance to go before she would meet Beaumont at the entrance to the park. He had promised to accompany her to the club. When her heart hammered against her waistcoat, she knew it was the thought of seeing Beaumont which was causing it to beat so, rather than the excitement of attending a gentlemen's club. What an adventure. She would confide to Mama all that occurred and was desperate not to miss out any detail as she would never again have the chance to relive it.

In her mind she had a vague notion as to what it might look like and pictured several dark wooden, well-polished tables dotted about a large room with comfortable armchairs arranged around them. Some of the members would be sipping claret and reading the newspapers while others smoked their cigarettes and cigars. At the thought of tobacco, Hope was immediately reminded of James Henderson. Goodness, what would happen if he were at the club? She felt jittery at the idea. It was too late now to worry about who might see her; no one would recognise her, especially if she was in the company of Beaumont. Perhaps she would find out a little more about this mysterious man. She had no idea who his friends were. Moving along the street, she almost collided with someone and was about to make an apology.

'Richard, how are you? Are you going to the club?' It was Beaumont, of course, putting himself into an actor's role.

Replying in kind, Hope said, 'Yes,

Beaumont. Shall we walk together?' It would be fine if he held her arm as they continued their journey. Oh dear, no it certainly would not! For an instant she had forgotten she was Richard rather than Hope. Her guard must not fall again for one moment.

Hope had no idea of their destination address and was surprised when Beaumont stopped walking and she almost bumped into him. Their physical contact had her nerve endings tingling again. 'Here we are at last. We can continue our conversation inside.'

As she followed Beaumont into the inviolate masculine haven, Hope tried not to stare, but it was impossible. She wanted to record every detail in her mind so she could write about it and draw it later in the privacy of her rooms.

Beaumont indicated that she stay near the door and he had a private word with someone who kept glancing at Hope until she felt like an exhibit at a museum or some such thing. Eventually, Beaumont returned to her side and directed her to a table which was just as she had imagined. Overjoyed, she sank into a deep armchair and looked about her.

'They were curious about you as you're not a member. I explained and now they think you're a dignitary visiting from France,' said Beaumont, his eyes dancing.

'This visit is an honour for me,' stated Hope.

'The honour is all mine,' declared Beaumont. 'Let me get you a drink. What do you prefer: port, whisky, brandy? And a cigar, I think.'

Hope could feel the colour drain from her cheeks at the thought. 'No, indeed,' she said, 'I do not smoke and rarely drink alcohol. Is there a cordial or coffee I may have?'

'I'm sure there is,' laughed Beaumont. He lifted a hand to the waiter and placed their order. 'What do you think of the exclusive gentlemen's club? Is it how you imagined it to be?'

'In some ways it is, yes. But what do

they do here? Apart from drink and read and smoke? Many of the members appear to be on their own. Why can't they remain at home?'

'They are in like company. Some live alone, like me. We come for companionship and also to dine. Isn't that why *we* are here?'

'Of course,' replied Hope. 'There's a lot to see too.' Hope looked around her again noticing the other gentlemen. Most of them were old and grey or old and bald, but there were a few younger ones.

'We shall ask for the menu when the waiter returns. Ah, here he is and he has one with him; he knows my habits well. Thank you, Canterbury.'

They leaned forward to read the selections for the day. Hope was aware of Beaumont's proximity which made her feel quite giddy. Would she ever get used to being near him? Then she remembered he had said he was going away. She nearly collapsed at the thought.

'Richard, are you quite well? You're trembling. Either you're hungry or you've a cold coming.'

'I, I expect I'm hungry, Beaumont,' Hope managed. 'What do you recommend?'

'The soup's good. I'm starting with that. Then I recommend either the roast pork or the chicken.'

'The soup will be adequate I feel sure.'

'Perhaps you will change your mind when your digestion gets working. Young men like you generally have good appetites.' Beaumont met her eyes with his and winked.

Shocked, Hope averted her gaze. Just then someone approached them and gabbled a garbled speech. It was all in French and she barely understood one word of it. She dared not risk a look at Beaumont. Whatever could she do? The gentleman paused in his monologue and waited, presumably for a reply.

'Richard is here to improve his English,' put in Beaumont smoothly.

'Pray don't ruin all his good intentions and make him revert to his mother tongue.'

'My apologies,' smiled the gentleman. 'I thought you'd like to converse in a language with which you were familiar.'

'That ees all right,' squeaked Hope. Then she cleared her throat and deepened her voice. 'It was a good gesture on your be'alf.'

'Mind if I join you, Beaumont?' asked the gentleman, about to pull out a chair to do just that.

'Sorry, we were about to go into the dining room. Please excuse us.' He stood and indicated to Hope that she should do the same. Trying to maintain a masculine bearing, Hope followed him.

It was as imposing as the rest of the club. The walls were panelled in dark wood and various portraits looked down on them. 'Who are these people?'

'That one at the end is the founder of the club; the others are benefactors and members who have been eminent in some way.'

'It's very grand.'

Beaumont looked as though he was going to pull her chair out for her. She caught his eye and gave a slight shake of her head.

'It's very difficult to remember when I am fully aware of your femininity. Even though you've had your hair cut I find you delectably womanly. In fact, I would proclaim it adds a je ne sais quoi to your whole character.'

Hope worriedly looked at the other diners and wondered if anyone would be able to hear their conversation.

'It is all right. We are far enough away from the others and the acoustics are not good. I have tried to hear conversations at times and failed.' He grinned at her. 'You did not expect that I would do such a thing. Or did you? What sort of a man do you think I am?'

It seemed easier to talk to him honestly now she was in the guise of Richard. Being a man freed her to communicate in a more open way.

'I think you are a man with a conscience. You question why you are fortunate and you want to help people less privileged than yourself. I think you are a good man. It is possible you are lonely too.' She put her hand to her mouth as though to stop further comments, but failed. 'I do not understand many things about you, but then I do not know you.'

Beaumont's hand reached out to touch hers, but he jerked it back. 'Oh, dear, this is very difficult. I will give the game away and we will be the talk of polite society. Will you mind?' His smile widened and he moved his chair an inch or so closer to Hope. Under the table his shining shoes sought out Uncle Eustace's ill-fitting boots and his knee pressed against her trouser leg. Hope felt her face suffusing with colour, but she would not move away. However, her companion did as Canterbury approached their table.

Hope looked about her while Beaumont ordered the meal. She almost pinched herself. How had she dared come here? What would Mama say? Would she laugh at her daughter's waywardness or would she finally disapprove of something her daughter had done? She hoped they would laugh together about it and she imagined describing the scene to her mother. Hope was quite sure *she* had never been inside a gentlemen's club.

Hope tried not to be too dainty as she tucked into the soup. It was comfortable sitting opposite Beaumont. There was no need to talk all the time and the food was good.

'Ah, you like our English cooking?'

Hope was taken aback. For a moment she had forgotten who she was meant to be. 'Mais, oui, it ees very good. Especially I like le rost bif here in your country.'

Beaumont laughed before saying, 'Then that is what you must have. As you have no stays or corsets or whatever it is women wear, you are free to eat as much as you like. I will forgo the chicken and have le rost bif as well.'

If any other man talked to her about women's undergarments she was sure she would feel somewhat embarrassed, but Beaumont was so direct about things it didn't seem to matter what he said. 'Sometimes I long to eat the full seven or eight courses, but as you say we are constricted by our garments. I have found wearing men's clothes frees me immensely.'

'And will you continue to dress as a man?'

'No, this is the very last time. These clothes are Uncle Eustace's and it would be dreadful should Aunt Constance discover what I have been doing. She has been very good about allowing me to teach the maids in the servants' hall.'

'The servants' hall? Wherever next? You are outrageous.' The twinkle in his eye told her that he didn't think so at all. It amused him. 'Tell me how you are teaching the maids and how well they are doing.'

It was very easy talking to Beaumont about her methods and how she planned to progress and he appeared to be genuinely absorbed.

'I think you are a natural teacher. I have been mulling over a similar idea. I would like to set up a school for adults who have had little chance to attend lessons and learn. It will open the door for them to the wonderful world of stories and possible opportunity for furtherance.'

'Like your magic lantern shows. Which reminds me. I have been thinking that a magic lantern show for Aunt Constance's servants at the house would be a special treat. We would provide the illustrated sheets too. Would that be possible before you leave?' She didn't want to think of Beaumont's departure as it was possible they would never meet again. She would almost certainly be back home with her parents if he returned to London.

'I would be delighted, but only if you have your aunt's permission. I am certainly not going to skulk round Eustace's house without his dear wife knowing I am there.'

Hope felt shamefaced. Beaumont's decency showed a flaw in her own character which she did not like at all.

11

Back at Aunt Constance's house, Hope wondered if the day had been a dream. Safely behind her own door, she sank onto the bed and pulled at the clothes which had clothed both Uncle Eustace and Richard. She meant what she'd said to Beaumont; this would definitely be the final time she wore them. Bouncing off the bed, she tore them from her and folded them neatly. They would have to be returned to her uncle's rooms. No, that wasn't possible as his other garments had been removed. Perhaps Edna would hide them until she had found another arrangement. That would remove the temptation of having them around.

A tap at her door told her Edna was coming to help her change her clothes yet again. She smiled as she thought of the times she'd done just that, but into those of a man. That would be behind her now.

'Edna, I have a favour to ask of you. Would you be able to take these clothes somewhere and prevent anyone from seeing them until I can think how they can be disposed of?'

The maid looked unhappy, but put on a little smile. 'If you wish, Hope. I think you know I'd do anything for you, especially after all the time and trouble you're going to in order to help us to read. The other servants are enjoying their lessons. They reckon you should be a teacher in a school. The way you explain things is easy to follow they say, and I agree with them.'

At the encouraging words, Hope felt cheered. What a wonderful day this was turning out to be. She allowed Edna to help her into a dress and tidy her hair. The two of them discussed the merits of short hair and Hope declared she loved being free of hair such as hers which had proved so unruly. It was a pity she couldn't disclose her latest exploit to Edna who would have enjoyed the gossip about the gentlemen's club, Hope was sure.

On a whim, Hope put her arms about her maid and hugged her. 'You are a lovely person, Edna. I'm pleased you're my maid. And thank you for all you do to help me.'

Edna blushed and pushed her mistress away gently, but not before returning the hug. 'Thank you, Hope. I'm pleased Her Grace asked me to attend you.'

Opening the door, Hope said, 'I'm going downstairs now, although I'm not at all hungry.' The reason for that, she kept to herself.

'Yes, my lady,' replied Edna politely. 'And I will do as you ask.' She indicated the pile of men's clothes on the bed.

★　★　★

After a night of deep slumber, Hope awoke with the sun streaming in through her opened drapes. She yawned and sat up in bed. 'What time is it, Edna? I trust I haven't overslept. I was so tired from . . .' Hope stopped and stared at the young servant in front of her. 'Who are you? No, wait a minute, I recognise you. You were in the servants' hall reading. Molly, isn't it?'

'Yes, your ladyship. Fancy you remembering my name. I mean, I'm sorry, I shouldn't talk to you like that.' Poor Molly looked so alarmed that Hope took pity on her.

'Really, you've done nothing wrong.' Hope pushed back the coverings and sat on the edge of her bed. 'Where's Edna? Is she ill?'

'I don't know, my lady. All I know is I was told to come and help you get ready for the day.' Molly looked around and went towards the cupboard where Hope's clothes were. 'What will you wear today? You have a lot of beautiful dresses, begging your pardon.'

Now Hope was worried; she couldn't bear the thought of Edna being so ill she was unable to attend to her. She must get ready quickly and find out what was causing her to be absent. 'I don't mind which I wear. Possibly the pink and green one, it's an old favourite.'

Molly did her best to help Hope look presentable enough to go downstairs, but her dress seemed ill-fitting and the fastenings stuck. Hastily looking at her reflection in the mirror, Hope said, 'Aunt Constance takes breakfast in her room usually so there will be no one to see me. Except Stevenson.'

'Yes, my lady.'

Hope hurried to breakfast to find Stevenson waiting for her arrival as usual. 'Good morning, Stevenson.'

'My lady,' bowed the butler.

Although Hope was anxious for news of Edna, she didn't want to appear too concerned about her; it wouldn't do for Stevenson to think they were close, although Hope felt he probably had a small idea of their rapport. 'A new maid came to me this morning. Is Edna quite well?'

'Edna doesn't work here any longer,' replied Stevenson, his voice not giving any weight to the words at all. He might as well have said that the weather was inclement or the eggs were ready.

'Whatever happened? Why did she leave?' Hope was sure Edna would never have done that without so much as a goodbye to her.

'You will have to ask Her Grace,' Stevenson informed her in a tone which indicated he was unwilling to say more.

'Very well.' Hope made sure she acted normally as she helped herself to breakfast and forced it down. She couldn't wait to speak to Aunt Constance.

She spent the morning unable to concentrate on any one thing. First she tried reading, then playing the piano, reading again and finally giving up she simply paced the rooms and hallway. Her aunt didn't appear until luncheon was served.

'What's the matter, Hope, dear? Have you lost your appetite?'

'I have rather. I am perplexed. My sweet maid, Edna, has apparently disappeared from the face of the earth and I am at a loss to know why.' Hope could feel tears forming.

'You shouldn't become so attached to the staff. I knew you were getting too close to the girl when you insisted she accompany you to the dressmaker and when you wanted to teach her to read.'

'I simply don't understand how she has left so suddenly and unexpectedly. Was she unhappy here?'

'She has been dismissed because she is a thief. Now let that be an end to it.'

That couldn't be true. Hope trusted Edna as much as she trusted her own maid at home. But even Ruth hadn't been expected to keep secrets as personal as those she'd shared with Edna. If she had been disloyal, surely she would have tittle-tattled.

'But, Aunt . . . ' Hope stopped when Aunt Constance glared at her.

'Hope, I have said that is an end to the matter. I do not expect to have to repeat myself. Now let us eat our lunch without further talk.'

After their meal Constance went out to visit an old friend and Hope paced the rooms again. Then she wrote in her journal with the desire that it would help her find a solution to her problem.

How is it possible Edna can be a thief? I refuse to believe what my aunt has said. There must be some mistake. What can I do? If Aunt Constance won't tell me anything further then the only person I can ask is Stevenson. Surely he can tell me. I will go and search him out before I lose my nerve.

Without thinking about it she headed for the back stairs and the butler's pantry. Stevenson was busy writing, but leapt to his feet as soon as he saw his visitor. 'Lady Hope, may I help you in anyway?'

'Yes, Stevenson you may. And I won't leave until you tell me the answer to my question. Why has Edna left?'

'At luncheon Her Grace was not prepared to tell you the details. Do you think I should do so against Her Grace's wishes?'

'I certainly do. I know Edna very well, as you do, and I do not for one moment believe she is a thief.'

'I will tell you what she did and you will know that we have both misjudged her character. One of the other servants saw her carrying a pile of clothes into their bedroom. She told the house-keeper who checked the room and found the clothes hidden under her mattress. They were His Grace's clothes and we believe she took them for members of her family. She was dismissed immediately. She will not get another position.'

Hope's heart sank at the news. 'May I see the clothes, Stevenson?'

'You may. I have put them in this cupboard.' He produced the clothes that Hope had worn and her heart sank a little further. 'Are you well, Lady Hope? You look somewhat pale. Here, let me get you something.'

Hope sipped at the drink and tried to

think how she would ever put things right. Her foolishness had meant poor Edna would no longer be able to support her family. What would become of them?

'Thank you, Stevenson,' she said weakly before making her way back to her bedroom. She looked at the trunk, then taking a deep breath opened it and pulled out the clothes which had been discarded as rags. She needed to talk to someone as she had no idea what to do about Edna's predicament and the only person she could think of who might possibly help was Beaumont. She was not going to involve Molly so she pulled out the hair pieces herself, dressed as a man and set off down the back stairs to escape.

The fresh air came to her aid as she hurried away from the house. Slowing her pace, she was able to think a little more clearly. She would go to the fair and if Beaumont wasn't there she would enquire where he lived. But he could be anywhere, possibly at the club.

Her attire was not suitable for a visit there. It was going to be a futile exercise, she felt sure. At least no one would recognise her dressed in the clothes which had been discarded as rags. However, when Hope compared them with the attire of some of the poor creatures she passed, she realised that her apparel was quite presentable. Perhaps she *could* go to the club after all, even if he wasn't there someone could tell her where he lived.

Having ascertained Beaumont's address, Hope quickly found her way to his street. She crossed the road without looking and there was a shout. She let out a light yelp before falling just short of a horse and carriage.

With her nose pressed to the grimy cobbles she was aware of only two things: someone was shouting and another person was bending down to tend her. It would not do for anyone to get close to her and discover her secret, so she bit her lip against the pain in her arm and made to stand.

'Stay where you are,' a voice commanded.

'All right,' murmured Hope, sinking back to the ground. She was safe now; the voice belonged to Beaumont.

His words came to her through a mist and she heard him instructing the carriage driver to go around the casualty who was not hurt badly. 'I'll take care of him, don't worry,' Beaumont assured the driver. 'I know him, he's a friend of mine.'

Hope felt a tingle rush through her as a moustache prickled her cheek and a puff of masculine breath blew softly into her ear. 'They've gone now. Get up if you can.'

'How did you know it was me?' demanded Hope, forgetting for the moment that this meeting was providential. All she could think of was the fact she'd been recognised.

'Your hat came off,' replied Beaumont, by way of explanation. 'Although I must admit your apparel did not give you away. Whatever are you wearing?'

She snatched the dilapidated hat and rammed it on her head. 'I came to find you.'

'I thought you said you were never going to dress as a man again.' Beaumont lowered his voice to a whisper although there was no one in hearing distance.

'It was an emergency,' said Hope. 'I owe you an explanation, but we can't talk here.'

'I agree. Would you come to my house? I saw the commotion from my window and came out to see what was happening.'

The house Hope walked into was unlike her aunt's in almost every respect. As she followed Beaumont along the hall, she was able to glimpse into the downstairs rooms. None appeared to be assigned for special purposes. In what she supposed was the dining room, a table vied with a piano and a chaise longue for space. And what Hope assumed to be the drawing room was filled with books and a table full of slides for the magic lantern. Various periodicals were strewn across surfaces. Hope smiled as she looked at the chaos.

'Something amuses you. Please tell me.'

Beaumont's eyes were steely, but they didn't deter Hope from saying, 'Have you a housekeeper?'

'Why do you ask? Are you worried about being chaperoned? I can assure you it doesn't matter as no one will know about your presence here and if anyone sees you they will assume you are a man.'

'I meant that you are most untidy, Beaumont!' Hope gasped at her own impudence.

Beaumont threw back his head and let out a roar of laughter. 'And you, my dear Hope, are very forthright. But that aside, please tell me what provoked you to change your decision and put on those very unbecoming clothes?'

With a sigh, Hope sank into a chair

and regaled Beaumont with the distressing story of Edna and finally came to the crux of the matter: her dismissal for something which was not her fault at all. She waited, feeling better for having been able to unburden herself. Beaumont would have the answer and things would return to normal.

To her dismay, he sat opposite her and stared at the wall for several minutes saying nothing at all. Hope's arm was throbbing a little, but she didn't dare take off her jacket to inspect it. She tried to sit still, waiting for Beaumont to break the silence. After a while she could bear it no longer, and stood up and walked from room to room, ideas flitting through her mind.

Wandering back to Beaumont, she was fast losing patience with him as he still appeared deep in thought. As she was on the verge of asking him if he had any ideas at all, he spoke. 'You will have to confess to Constance.'

This was what Hope had dreaded. She knew it was the correct thing to own up to her aunt, but she also expected it would put her in a bad humour which would not help Edna at all. After she explained to Beaumont, he nodded. 'But it has to be done. There's been enough duplicity.'

'You are right,' admitted Hope. 'I know you are. At first I was hesitant to confront my aunt because of what she would think of me, but at the moment I care more about Edna than myself.'

'Very commendable. But if Edna is to get a fair hearing, Constance must know the whole story.'

With the decision made, Beaumont accompanied Hope to her aunt's house so she could enter unobtrusively while he was talking to Constance.

When she had changed into a dress and fixed a hair piece, Hope went to find her aunt, anticipating Beaumont would still be with her.

'Hope, you're flushed and out of breath, what have you been up to?' Aunt Constance frowned at her niece.

'Nothing much,' replied Hope, avoiding Beaumont's amused gaze.

'As I was saying, Constance, I wish you would let me have Hope's help to create some slides for a new show I have in mind. She has shown herself to be talented in many ways.' At this he placed himself firmly in front of Hope so she had no way of politely avoiding his eyes which were shining above a barely-concealed grin.

'Certainly, Beaumont. As you are both here now, can you set to work? It doesn't appear that Hope has much to do at the moment and she certainly needs distracting.'

'Are you suggesting I distract your niece?' queried Beaumont. 'However,' he continued, without waiting for a reply, 'I think it best if she could come to my house as I have all the equipment there. Would that be possible to arrange?'

'No doubt it could be. I will let you know when I am able to chaperone her.'

'I beg your pardon, Hope,' said

Beaumont incomprehensibly. Whatever did he mean, she wondered. 'I thought you were about to say something.'

Now she understood and took a deep breath. 'Yes, I was. Something important. Aunt Constance I am guilty of a gross transgression.'

As she stammered and stuttered her way through the story from the start to the end, her aunt's face set deeper and deeper into a frown. When Hope finished with the latest part about going to Beaumont's house for advice, there was an interminable silence. She paced the room, occasionally glancing at her aunt and Beaumont who seemed to be transfixed by a painting of one of Uncle Eustace's ancestors.

'Sit down, Hope, you are wearing me out with your pacing.'

'Yes, Aunt.' Hope immediately did as her aunt commanded.

'You took your dead uncle's clothes to wear?'

'Yes, Aunt.'

'And you went out in them, either

with Edna or on your own?'

'Yes, I confess I did.'

'You went to the fair and to a gentlemen's club?'

'Yes, dear Aunt.'

'You walked in the park alone.'

'I did.'

'Whatever will your mother say?'

'I think she will pretend to be cross, but I think she will also wish she had been to a gentlemen's club. She has often wondered what they are like.'

Beaumont spluttered. 'Excuse me, Constance, I appear to have a tickle in my throat.' When Hope glanced at him he winked at her yet again. She winked back which had him spluttering even more. Hope realised she shouldn't be so frivolous, yet what did it matter that she had worn men's clothes? Nothing awful had befallen her. Then she remembered that they had been her dead uncle's clothes. That *did* make her feel uncomfortable.

'I do not know what to say or think.' Constance tapped her fingers on the table. 'I am considering how Eustace would have regarded the matter. What do you think, Beaumont? What would your esteemed ally have said?'

'It isn't my place to say. You knew him better than I did, better than anyone else in the world. You are the only one who would be able to say how he would react to Hope's behaviour and mine. I have to tell you that I have played a part in the events. I encouraged Hope to come to the fair a second time and to my club.'

'I am aware of your at times shocking behaviour, Beaumont. It is part of the reason Eustace liked you.' Constance appeared lost in thought again.

Beaumont looked at Hope and smiled weakly, before addressing her aunt again. 'Have you thought yet how he would react to Hope wearing his clothes?'

Constance's face lit up. 'He would have laughed and told her she should use a more competent tailor. He was an elegant man, do you remember?'

'Indeed I do. I remember the time he told me that he would take me to his tailor as my jacket was ill-fitting.'

'I was somewhat askance when I discovered the ragged clothing in Eustace's rooms until I remembered he sometimes liked to stray incognito outside the house to see how the underprivileged lived,' said Constance.

'Indeed, I can testify to that. He earned my great respect because he wanted to witness for himself the poverty experienced by many in the city,' replied Beaumont. 'He looked a remarkable sight in those clothes.'

Constance laughed. 'Dear, dear, Eustace. I miss him dreadfully.'

When her aunt's laughter turned into huge sobs, and tears rolled down her cheeks, Hope leapt from her place and rushed over to hug her. 'Dear Aunt, I am very sorry to cause you such unhappiness. I am afraid my impetuousness will be my undoing. Papa always says so. Please, have my handkerchief.'

'Thank you. I know there is no need to apologise to either of you for my behaviour as neither of you is bound by propriety.'

Beaumont walked over and rested his hand on her shoulder. 'I think you have been holding back your feelings, Constance, and therefore have not grieved properly. I also think Hope would like to know what you will be doing about her indiscretions.'

'Nothing, I will do nothing. You are a good natured and kind young woman, Hope. Your mother has brought you up well in spite of her casual nature. I adored my brother when we were growing up, still do, and I see your personality in him. He's a good father to you, I have no doubt. If Eustace and I had been blessed with children I would have liked them to be as high spirited as you.'

'Oh, dear Aunt, I will try hard to behave properly for the rest of my stay with you. But first we must find Edna and bring her back as she has been wrongly accused of theft and she told me her family depend on her for their livelihood.'

'I suppose you will be gallivanting round the poor parts of London searching for her!' Constance chuckled.

'I will search Edna out,' Beaumont said, 'there is no need for Hope to leave here.'

'No, Hope must go too. She has caused Edna to be sent away. She must go and fetch her back. I suggest you go and dress in Eustace's clothes and go with Beaumont to find the maid. That way you will have no need of a chaperone. But before you change we will ring for Stevenson and see if he knows her whereabouts.'

'We will try not to walk in the path of a carriage this time, won't we Hope?'

'What's this? You did not mention a carriage.'

'Hope almost stepped in the path of a carriage and fell to the ground when she was coming to ask me for my advice.'

'You poor girl. Did you hurt yourself?'

Hope had been trying very hard not to allow the pain in her arm to trouble her. In fact she had regarded it as punishment for what she had done. But as her aunt and Beaumont looked at her sympathetically tears formed in her eyes.

'My dear girl.' Constance and Beaumont were immediately at her side, encouraging her to sit down and asking where the pain was worse.

'I fell down with my arm beneath me. It feels bruised, but I'm sure it's nothing.'

'I insist you show me, Hope,' commanded Aunt Constance, now back to her sterner self.

Hope reluctantly turned back the cuff on her sleeve and a livid bruise showed itself. Beaumont took her hand and inspected the injury.

'There is no sign of a cut, but the discolouration and lump I can see tell me you must be in agonising pain.' His fingers ran over her flesh causing her to quiver. 'But I'm hurting you,' he murmured. 'And that's the very last thing I wish to do.'

'No, you're not at all,' replied Hope, enjoying his touch and wanting it to last for ever. Then she was aware of her aunt's gaze on her arm.

'It does look tender, dear. I suppose it is impossible that you should go through all the adventures you have without suffering in some way.' Then Constance pursed her lips and asked, 'Is there anything else I haven't been told?'

'Yes, Aunt, there is one thing.' Hope pulled the grips from her hair and tugged the hair piece out. 'I had my hair cut short.'

Constance shook her head. 'I will go and lie down. I trust you, Beaumont, to look after my niece and bring both her and Edna safely home.'

12

Having ascertained Edna's address, Hope and Beaumont jostled their way along streets and narrow alleyways until they found it. Hope was amazed at the layout of the areas off the main roads. She had often wondered what the poorer areas looked like and now she knew. Dressed in Uncle Eustace's ragged clothes, she tried to imagine what his thoughts might have been as he traversed these back alleys. And had Beaumont been with him? She longed to ask him, but her arm was throbbing, her heart was racing and she had myriad thoughts crossing her mind. Just as she was about to request Beaumont to slow his pace, he stopped and pointed. 'This is it.' He raised his fist and rapped on the wooden door.

Edna answered his knock and appeared to almost faint when she glimpsed him and her erstwhile mistress. Hope bent forward and embraced the young girl. 'You were wrongly accused and you said nothing.'

'What could I have said?' replied Edna. 'It would have been my word against yours. And I think very highly of you, my lady; I wouldn't have wanted any trouble for you.'

Beaumont raised his hat and said, 'I think Hope has something to say.'

'I've confessed to Aunt Constance. She knows what I did. That I dressed as a man in Uncle Eustace's clothes. Her reaction has astounded me, but I think I'm forgiven or at least on the way to being. I begged that you be allowed to return to your job in her household and she is agreeable.'

'I'm not sure about that,' began Edna.

'Don't let pride get the better of you,' cautioned Beaumont with the wave of his hand. 'Think of your family. Employment brings in money.' He peered behind Edna into the darkness of her home. 'How many of you are reliant on your wages? Too many, I'll warrant. Why don't you get your belongings and return?'

'Do you mean I should come back immediately with you?' asked Edna.

Hope considered the question. Edna had been wronged and she must not be bullied into submission. 'Come when you are ready,' she said. 'I'm looking forward to you being with me again. We will explain to Aunt Constance you will arrive soon.'

Edna gave a broad smile and shut the door.

★　★　★

Back at Aunt Constance's house, Beaumont waited while Hope changed into a dress. As she descended the stairs her head whirled. She'd had so many escapades in the past days and she felt quite disorientated. If only Mama were here, she thought. She told herself the tears which threatened were on account of the pain in her arm and the relief of Edna returning to the household, but in truth that was not the whole reason. Aunt Constance had surprised her with her reactions to almost everything during this sojourn with her. Uncle Eustace and she must have shared a remarkably close relationship; rather like Mama and Papa, she supposed. If only she could find a companion with whom she could experience that intimacy. Briefly, she thought of Isabella and James Henderson. Would they be close? Or would they perhaps marry and become distant with each other after a time?

The sound of humming made her smile. It was Beaumont. Just like her aunt, he never ceased to amaze her. He must be a busy person, yet he had given no thought to accompanying her to persuade Edna back. And now he was awaiting her.

'Thank you for helping me to make things right between myself and my aunt. I am indebted to you.' Hope grinned and gave a mock curtsy.

'You are a terrible woman, Hope Richmond,' sighed Beaumont approaching her. 'You haven't even bothered to attach a hair piece.'

Hope's hand snaked up to her head and she gasped. 'I forgot. Do you think it matters now that Aunt Constance knows I've been wicked and cut my hair?'

'I don't care what Constance knows or doesn't know at this moment. My concern is what you look like.'

'I thought you were of the opinion that short hair became me,' objected Hope, feeling a bit unwell at the thought of incurring Beaumont's wrath.

'That's the trouble,' said Beaumont, his voice husky as if he were coming down with a cold. 'It becomes you too well.' He came towards her, cupped her face in his hands and delicately brought his lips to hers. As she felt the bristles against her mouth, she felt sure she would fall to the floor. This was far more than she'd ever dared to wish for.

Thoughts of her mama, Aunt Constance and anybody else drained from her as she gave herself up to the ecstasy of Beaumont's embrace.

★   ★   ★

Beaumont took his leave shortly afterwards and Hope was confident nothing on the whole earth could make her more happy than the thought of the kiss they'd shared. She fled up the stairs to her rooms and flung herself on the bed reliving over and over their intimate time together. It had been but a moment, yet it had seemed endless. There was no way she could keep the smile off her face and she felt it best if she remain in her room for as long as she could because if she met her aunt she was sure to give herself away. Bouncing off the bed, she examined her appearance in the mirror. Her eyes were shining and her lips were tingling. As she reminisced about why that was, she saw herself blushing.

Then she heard a commotion coming from downstairs and shortly afterwards there was a loud knock at her door. When she opened it, Molly stood there jumping from one foot to the other. 'Please, my lady, Her Grace asks that you come downstairs immediately. Begging your pardon.' Molly bobbed her head and hurried off.

Oh dear, thought Hope. What have I done now?

As she entered the drawing room she could not believe her eyes. 'Mama!'

'Hope!' Her mother held her arms wide and Hope rushed into them.

'Is it really you? I thought you were still in Italy.'

'I wrote to tell you I was coming back. I expect the letter will turn up sometime. Let me look at you.'

Hope stepped back and self-consciously tried to tidy her hair.

'It suits you. Your aunt has told me a little of what has been going on. It seems that your stay in London has been more exciting than you could have wished.'

'I have so much to tell you, Mama, but where is Papa? Is he here with you?'

'No, he was invited to give some lectures which meant we would be staying away for much longer than we'd planned. I thought it was a good opportunity to return home and see you. And to ensure Constance would be willing to give you a home for some time longer.'

'I am very pleased you are here.' Hope glanced at her aunt, trusting she hadn't hurt her feelings. 'Aunt Constance has been wonderful of course, but I have missed you.'

Constance smiled. 'Let us have tea and then I will leave you, Prudence, to catch up on all your daughter's exploits. I wanted to introduce her to some of the most eligible men in London, but I am very much afraid she has befriended someone most unsuitable. As well as being older than she is, he is . . . how shall I put it . . . unconventional.'

'How fascinating.' Prudence took her

daughter's hand and squeezed it reassuringly.

* * *

'He sounds exciting, this Beaumont without a title. I am very much looking forward to making his acquaintance.'

'Please, Mama, don't make too much of him. I have told you about him because I like him and we share many interests, but Beaumont and I are friends only and he is travelling to Yorkshire soon for business.' Hope felt herself colouring as she remembered their kiss. Would they have kissed if they were only friends?

'As you will be staying in London longer than expected he has plenty of time to come back and for you to get to know each other better if I find that he is a suitable beau for my precious daughter. We must attend one of his magic lantern shows. I am pleased Constance hasn't been too concerned with the correctness expected in London society and has allowed you a certain amount of latitude.'

'She has been astonishing and I think she is starting to recover from her grief. They must have been a wonderful couple. I didn't know Uncle Eustace very well, but I wish I had as he was much concerned about the poor and went about in ragged clothing to find out about their lives.'

'Really? That I never knew. He was a remarkable man and they truly loved each other.'

'And poor Papa had to battle in order to marry you.'

'Yes, he was expected to marry a neighbour's daughter. She was an earl's daughter like you, but as unlike you in personality as anyone could possibly be. But your dear father and I met at a ball and fell in love. Of course, I was quite unsuitable being the daughter of an untitled gentleman. Your father is determined when he thinks something is worth fighting for and finally we were allowed to marry and eventually I was accepted into the family. I think Constance grew to like me when we knew each other better.' Her mother paused. 'I am very pleased to be here and know that you are well and enjoying yourself. We felt guilty about our wonderful trip when we thought of you.'

'I expect I will have plenty of opportunity to travel, but at the moment I am more than happy.'

'We must write to your father and let him know. Now tell me more about how the maids are doing with their learning. And have you heard from Ruth at all?'

After answering her mother's question and telling her about the maids' lessons, Hope went to her room and reached for her journal. She had much to write about.

Mama and I have talked at length and still have plenty to tell each other. She has told me something of the impressive galleries and buildings they have seen and made me laugh when she described characters they have come across. I told her she should have been an actress and she looked wistful and said that it is what she would have most liked to be, but how unsuitable it would have been. Seeing that look of longing in her eyes has made me think that maybe she will let me follow my desire to teach. She is enthusiastic about the lessons I have been giving the maids and says she will join me in the servants' hall next time I take a class. What will Stevenson think to that? It has been a wonderful day and to make it perfect I received a letter from Ruth.

Hope paused to re-read the short letter from Ruth which was adorned with crossings out and smudges.

Dear Hope,
    I trust this letter finds you well and in good spirits. Mother and Father are both well now and the rest of the family have not cort the influenza. I

wud like to return to you as soon as you go home if that wud be akseptible. Is my speling good?
    Ruth

Hope smiled affectionately at the letter before resuming writing in her journal.

It is marvellous Ruth has the confidence to write to me and I will make sure she receives the praise she deserves although it might be quite a while before I return home. My feelings are mixed. I would like to spend some time with Mama and Papa at home, but on the other hand, by staying in London I may have the opportunity to see Beaumont if he returns as Mama suggests he might. How I long to spend time with him.

A repeated tapping on the door stopped her flow of thought. Had Molly come to tell her Beaumont was awaiting her downstairs?

When the maid entered all thought of Beaumont flew from her head as it was Edna, not Molly, standing before her.

'Edna, how delighted I am to see you.' She went to her maid, took both her hands and smiled. 'Do you forgive me?'

'There is nothing to forgive. I have enjoyed more excitement since you have lived here than in the whole of the rest of my life.'

'I think that may be an exaggeration, but we have enjoyed some stirring exploits together. My day is complete now you have returned. The other great event of today is that my dearest mama has come to stay.'

'All the way from Italy?' Edna's eyes widened.

'Yes, but she will be returning to re-join my papa after her visit here. She would like to meet Beaumont and attend a magic lantern show. Oh, Edna, I can't stop talking about him.'

'If you will excuse me for saying so, I believe you are taken with him. Possibly even a little in love with him.'

'I think you may be quite right.' Hope sighed.

'Have you told your mother about everything? Your hair and dressing up as Richard?'

'Indeed I have and she has taken it all very well. She also told me she always wanted to be an actress.'

Edna's hand flew to her mouth.

'It's quite shocking, don't you think? Edna, you must keep that information to yourself. As Aunt Constance says, we wouldn't want Lady Padstock to hear.'

'No, I won't say a word, you can trust me.'

'I know I can. You didn't say a word about why you had Uncle Eustace's clothes. You protected me and for that I will always think well of you. Now how would you like a reading lesson?'

'That would be very nice.'

'I will go and find Mama as she would like to join us. Do not be shy with her, please. She will be a great help to us. We will see if Stevenson welcomes her into the servants' hall.'

The two women giggled together before Hope went in search of her mother and met her on the landing just as she was about to descend the stairs.

'Edna has returned and I am going to give her and the other maids a lesson. Would you join us?'

'I would be delighted.' Her mother looked at her then at the banisters and before anyone could say 'Stevenson' they had both clambered onto the banister and were shooting downstairs, squealing as they went.

'I believe I arrived first, Hope.' Prudence smoothed down the skirt of her gown and pushed a tendril of hair behind her ear.

'Next time, Mama, I will be first.'

'Never!'

★　★　★

Hope sat quietly at the dinner table as her aunt and mother talked of mutual friends and acquaintances. Her thoughts ran to Beaumont. What was he doing at this moment? Was he thinking of her just as she was of him? When would she see him again? She would tell him of this afternoon's lesson and introduce him to her mama who would fall under his spell. Her aunt's voice brought her to the present.

'It is delightful to have you staying here, Prudence. With the company of you and your enchanting daughter I am sure I will soon be back to my former strength. Meantime my physician says I must rest. I will not be entertaining or making calls, but please regard my home as your own and entertain as you see fit.'

'When did you see the physician, Aunt?'

'Several weeks ago.'

'And he said complete rest?'

'Yes.'

'My dear Aunt, you have been persevering with social activities because of me.'

'I have, Hope, but it was not your

fault. I have instilled in me a sense of duty. You were entrusted into my care and I did not wish to let you down. Now I will rest in my room. Prudence, I would like you to take on the running of the house. It does not require much thought on my part as Stevenson and the housekeeper have been here for many years. I simply request that you do not turn my home into a public library or school.' With a smile Constance kissed them both and left the room.

'Poor Aunt Constance. I feel dreadful, Mama, especially as I haven't been an easy guest.'

'She has a stout constitution like your father. I am sure with rest she will soon be back to her former self. I believe she put on a brave face and didn't grieve properly for Eustace.'

'The Queen has also found the loss of her husband unbearable, hasn't she?'

'The trouble is when one finds an exceptional companion then the loss of that companion is almost more than one can bear. I simply can't imagine life without your father. He is my other half and thus makes me whole. I hope that one day you too will find someone to love like that. Maybe you already have.'

Hope could feel her cheeks growing hot. 'I don't know. I have spent so little time with Beaumont, yet when we are together I feel as though I can be myself. I don't have to be the Earl's daughter.'

'I wish to meet him soon. If he proves to be unsuitable, well . . . I would like you to be guided by my opinion. Let us not even consider that. I am sure if you find him agreeable and stimulating company then I will too.'

'But what about Beaumont? I am uncertain as to his feelings. One minute I think he likes me,' the passionate kiss vividly returned to her mind, 'and the next he says he is unworthy and wants to leave London.'

'He is certainly a mystery, but one we will get to the bottom of. Shall we visit him tomorrow?'

'Is that quite right and proper, Mama?'

'Definitely not, but do you think your Beaumont will mind?'

★ ★ ★

'Please excuse all the clutter,' Beaumont said as he waved his hand vaguely at his drawing room. He lifted a pile of magazines from the sofa and invited Prudence and Hope to be seated. 'May I offer you some refreshments?'

'If you feel it is not unseemly then a large whisky each would be very nice.'

Hope's spluttering at her mother's behaviour turned into a bad fit of coughing. Her mother patted her on the back. Beaumont didn't seem at all daunted by the request.

'May I please have a cup of tea instead?' Hope asked.

'Of course. I will ring for my housekeeper. Meanwhile I would enjoy hearing of your travels.'

As Mama talked, Hope watched

Beaumont. He appeared genuinely interested in the stories and listened raptly. When the drinks arrived the conversation turned to magic lanterns and slides.

'When can we expect to hold the show for Constance's servants?' Prudence asked. 'As she is laid low we may have it when we wish, I don't need to bother her with it.'

'I am quite happy to do it anytime, but Hope wanted to make some slides to go with her own story, did you not?'

'I did. I have written the story. When would it be possible to start on the slides?'

'I have no appointments today. I will order luncheon to be served later, so shall we start now? These are the glass slides on which you paint. It is a very delicate process. This paint is of a special type and the brushes sometimes have only one bristle, like this one.' Beaumont held up a brush for the two women to inspect. 'You may wish to use a magnifying glass for very small images. When the picture is dry we will put another piece of glass over it and join the two together.'

Hope enjoyed the delicacy of the work and painstakingly tried to produce something of worth. It was far more satisfying than embroidery.

'I have made a mistake with mine.' Prudence sighed with impatience. 'I felt I was making progress. It is too fiddly for me. When I paint I like a large canvas and dramatic flourishes.'

'Indeed, I am sorry. I can see that Hope is devoted to detail. This slide is quite perfect.' Beaumont held the slide Hope had painted up to the light and studied it. Hope watched him and he turned to smile at her.

'You have many gifts, Hope.' Beaumont looked at her with admiration.

'She is an eligible young woman, Beaumont, but is rather too unconventional for most suitors. I blame myself for that characteristic as I too am unconventional which is one of the reasons why I am leaving the two of you to your slides as soon as we have eaten luncheon. The other reason is that I could not spend a minute longer attempting to produce a useable slide. Your housekeeper will be present.'

Even Hope was surprised that her mother was prepared to leave her alone with Beaumont at his house, but it suggested to her that she approved of him. Her heart fluttered when she thought of what might happen during the afternoon as they worked together in close proximity.

'There is an exhibition which I desire to see, as does an old friend. I will return for you in the late afternoon, Hope.'

Hope tried to slow her racing heart. A whole afternoon alone with Beaumont was more than she could have dreamed of.

* * *

Sitting at the small table positioned by the window in the drawing room, Hope and Beaumont worked in silence.

'I failed to tell your mother that my housekeeper has the afternoon off. Was that very wrong of me?' His eyes twinkled.

'Quite wrong, Beaumont.' Hope smiled at him and he took her hand and held it gently.

'You are in safe hands. I would do nothing to harm you or your reputation.'

'I know.' She didn't care for her reputation or anything else. Hope longed for him to take her in his arms and kiss her as rapturously as he had before, but instead he simply raised her hand to his lips, kissed it then let her go.

She continued with her intricate painting, but she was trembling now. His presence so close to her had an effect she was unable to quell. Did Beaumont feel the same?

The afternoon passed pleasantly enough, but with no talk of feelings and no passionate embraces.

Back at Aunt Constance's house, Hope confided in her journal.

Today has been extraordinary. Mama likes Beaumont. She thinks he is an 'intriguing, kind and striking man'. She would like to get to know him better and has suggested we go cycling in the park. Beaumont says he will borrow two bicycles from friends as he already has one. It is great fun with Mama here and I no longer have to hide my activities.

And do I now know what Beaumont thinks of me? Although we were alone together all afternoon, he didn't attempt to kiss me and I didn't try to kiss him. Maybe next time we meet I should do so and see how he reacts.

I can't wait for tomorrow. We are meeting Beaumont in Hyde Park where we will see if we have remembered how to bicycle, and have a picnic. It would be nice if the sun shone, but our enjoyment will not be governed by the weather. I think Mama will have too much fun to leave us alone again.

Lying on the grass under a tree watching the sunshine dappling the ground, Hope felt content. The cycling had been tremendous fun and the picnic delicious. Beaumont was sitting leaning against a tree trunk, his eyes closed with a cheerful expression on his face. Mama was walking round the pond in the distance.

Beaumont opened his eyes and broke the silence. 'Hope, we must make a decision.'

'We must.' She felt sure he was about to declare himself, state that he had fallen in love with her and he would approach Papa on his return.

'When will we hold the magic lantern show at Constance's house?'

'Oh.' She recovered herself quickly. 'Whenever you like.'

'It must be soon. We will see if Prudence will agree to an evening this week.'

'Yes, of course.' Why had she

expected him to talk of anything else? The kiss must have been a mistake which he now regretted.

'It looks as though your mother is in a hurry.' He indicated her returning figure then stood and brushed some bark from his clothes.

'You must come, both of you. There are rowing boats to hire. They are such fun. Please say you'll come with me.'

Beaumont raised his eyebrows at Hope and together they rushed to catch up with Prudence who was already half way back to the lake.

'I would like to row,' Prudence announced.

'I would too,' Hope added.

'Then I will sit at leisure and you can each take an oar.'

On the way home, Hope recalled the relaxed atmosphere of their time together. Beaumont had been very good company. He hadn't interfered in the wishes of her or Mama at all. In fact, he had enhanced their enjoyment by letting them bicycle and picnic. Many gentlemen would have insisted on rowing the boat, but Beaumont had merely sat back and let them take charge.

13

Hope couldn't contain her joy. Not knowing quite what to do with herself she sat at the escritoire and wrote in her journal.

It is a most thrilling time. Beaumont will be here shortly to set up the magic lantern in the rearranged servants' hall. I have been busy finishing the slides for my story and I am surprisingly pleased with them as this was my first attempt. Beaumont has not seen them all and I wish for him to find them pleasing. There has been a great deal of anticipation amongst the servants. Mama has ordered refreshments for the interval and even Stevenson seems to have a little spring in his step.

And what is more I have written an article and sent it to a magazine. After much deliberation I sent it in my own

name rather than a masculine pseudonym. I long for it to be accepted. I feel
as though all sorts of doors are opening
for me.

The only fly in the ointment is
Beaumont's departure to the north. I
wish he could be dissuaded from going,
but I doubt that is possible. Mama will
leave me too as soon as she is satisfied
Aunt Constance is completely recovered. Thus far she has remained in her
room which worries us. I do not relish
the thought of both Mama and
Beaumont deserting me, although my
aunt is good company when she is well.

I gave Edna and some of the other
maids another short lesson this morning and they are quick at learning as
well as being delightful company. They
chatter and giggle all the way through,
but learn more quickly that way I think
than if I made them be silent and
serious.

Of course, not all the servants are
illiterate. Stevenson has professed he
learned his reading and writing skills

from the butler some time ago, and I have observed the housekeeper reading from a newspaper. I even witnessed a short conversation between her and the cook in French. To my shame, it surprised me. I must be more open-minded.

★   ★   ★

As Hope surveyed the transformed servants' hall she gave a sigh of satisfaction. Mama was seated on the front row of chairs and there was a gentle anticipatory chatter from the servants who had all been given leave to attend. Stevenson sat on the back row listening for any call to duty from the bellboard. Hope sorted her music at the upright piano in the corner. She had wanted one of the servants to play, but they had all been too shy although she knew one or two of them were competent.

Beaumont walked to her side. 'Ready?'
'Yes and thank you, Beaumont. This

is a marvellous undertaking.'

'Let's begin.' He indicated to Molly to turn out the last of the lamps when everyone's attention was taken by a commotion at the door. Constance swished into the room, nodded at Stevenson, smiled at Beaumont and Hope and sat in the vacant seat next to Prudence.

The show began and by the interval any anxiety Hope had been feeling was gone. The enthusiasm of the servants for the stories Beaumont had shown had been overwhelming and she was particularly pleased with the reaction to her own story. The kitchen maids served a selection of drinks, bread and cheese and little groups gathered to discuss the show.

Hope was surprised there were so many people present. She knew her aunt had an enormous house and extensive grounds, but she hadn't met all the staff. Some she recognised, of course, but she would like to find out who the others were.

As Hope meandered through the gathering she heard Edna say, 'I recognised you, Molly. I'm sure one of the slides had you in it.'

Molly blushed and nodded. 'I thought so, too. Will I be famous, do you think?' The two friends giggled together and helped themselves to some of the food.

Other servants were poring over the pamphlets Hope had made depicting the story. 'It's lovely to be able to have these as a reminder of the show.'

'I'll never forget it for as long as I live,' breathed one of the other maids. 'I've heard about the magic lantern shows, but I could never afford to go to the music hall or fair and see one.'

Hope felt her cheeks burn as she recalled she'd entered the premises without payment. But perhaps the show they'd put on today compensated for that indiscretion.

Everywhere she turned, Hope heard compliments flying about the performance. It was most rewarding.

Stevenson approached. 'My lady,

may I express my gratitude for the show. The servants needed to be lifted out of their gloom. Since the death of His Grace, a certain melancholy descended over the house. Until you arrived, that is.' He gave a cough and made to walk away.

Hope gave him a wide smile. 'I fear my presence has unnerved everyone. I seem to bring chaos.'

'On the contrary, we have noticed a distinct change in Her Grace since your arrival, even though she has had to retire to her rooms again. It is good to see her with us this evening. Initially I feared your presence would upset the household, but I was quite wrong. You have lifted everyone's spirits.'

'I trust attending this evening won't be too much for her.' Hope was worried now and glanced over at her aunt. She seemed to be at ease and relaxed chatting to her sister-in-law and Beaumont. Perhaps she really was improving in health.

At the end of the show Constance

stood and clapped her hands together for silence. 'From your reaction I think you have all enjoyed the magic lantern show.' She was interrupted by a burst of applause. 'I would like to thank not only Beaumont and my niece, Lady Hope, for their work, but also my dear sister-in-law, Lady Richmond, for giving permission in my absence. I have an idea that we shall have monthly entertainments.' Again cheers and clapping stopped her briefly from proceeding. 'Possibly a concert next month. I have caught some of you singing as you work and I believe there are some pianists amongst you. Stevenson, I will leave you in charge of the arrangements.'

'Yes, Your Grace. I could possibly demonstrate my skill with the spoons.'

Some of the maids tittered behind their hands before they started clearing away the dirty china.

Hope could barely contain herself. 'Beaumont, thank you. It went better than I could have wished and I am very pleased Aunt Constance felt well enough to join us.' She watched her aunt and mother as they left the room to return upstairs.

'It was very satisfying and it seems your aunt has decided she will follow our example and provide entertainment for members of the household. Some households hold a weekly dance, but best not to run before we can walk.'

Hope's feelings were out of control. She wanted to reach up and kiss his luscious lips and run her hands through his hair. She longed for the feel of his body against hers, but she could do nothing except talk. 'When are you leaving us?'

'Tomorrow.'

Hope felt Beaumont's hand take hers and her body felt like blancmange. It was such a light, delicious touch, it meant the world to her. Instilled with confidence, she began, 'Beaumont, before you go, would you please tell me why you are a man with no title? Do you merely mean that you are not a nobleman? Because if that is the dilemma, I assure you it isn't always deemed to be a bad thing. My own mother came from an untitled family and not even Aunt Constance frowns on that now she's acquainted with her.'

Beaumont stared at the wall behind Hope for a long time and she feared she would not obtain a reply. She fidgeted while she waited. He'd dropped her hand and she was sure she'd offended him. Just as she was about to apologise and change the subject, he said, 'Anyone who is a lord, an earl or any other sort of noble must behave with dignity and set a good example. I believe that to be true of *all* people.' His eyes were upon her now and she was mesmerised by both them and his words. 'I have been privileged. I have never gone cold or hungry and I have always had a roof over my head. Because of that, I should have helped those who have far less.'

When he paused, Hope jumped in. 'Beaumont, of course you've helped people. The poor are always uppermost in your thoughts and see how you have brought not only enjoyment, but also education to the gathering of the servants today. Also, I know you have donated money from your magic lantern shows to charities and then there are the food parcels you regularly send out, not to mention . . . ' Hope trailed off as she regarded the unhappy expression on his face.

'It is not enough,' he asserted.

'Well then, what would make it enough?' demanded Hope. She couldn't bear to see his tortured soul laid bare like this. He was a good, strong man with much influence. Why on earth would he think he wasn't worthy?

'If I thought I was indispensable, I suppose.' He gave a forced laugh which tore through Hope's heart. 'But that makes me self-regarding.'

'Which in turn makes you unworthy? Beaumont, it appears you have lessons to learn as well as give.' Hope could so very easily have told him in truth that he was vital to her, but intuitively she felt he had to find that out for himself. She strode from the room before he could see her much too-bright eyes.

* * *

Hope wasn't sure if she was more cross or upset. It was a puzzle to her why Beaumont should regard himself as he did. There must be more to it than he had divulged. Perhaps she shouldn't have stormed off as she had. A knock at her door interrupted her thoughts.

'Can I come in, darling?' Dear Mama. How very welcome she was.

'Oh, Mama, I have behaved appallingly when I should have been patient and understanding. Now I don't know what to do.'

Prudence laughed and pulled Hope onto the bed beside her, giving her such a hug that it was difficult to breathe. It was comforting to inhale the sweetness of her mother's skin. She felt safe and loved. After a while, her mother murmured, 'Tell your mama what is troubling you. I'm sure we can find a solution.' She listened as Hope unburdened herself. Unsure whether she should disclose that she was falling in love with Beaumont, she held back some of the details. However, her mama could read her mind it would seem. 'So, darling Hope, you have fallen deeply in love with Beaumont.'

'Oh, Mama, what shall I do? I hate to see him unhappy; I don't want him to go away. I don't know what to do.'

Prudence gently took her arms from around her daughter and stood up. She walked to the window and looked out. With her back to Hope, she said, 'I may have the solution to the problem. I remember your father and Constance discussing someone. At the time I had no idea who it was, but I'm sure I'm right when I think of it now. I believe Beaumont is concerned with the sins of the father as mentioned in the Bible. Although in his case, it would be the grandfather. He was a tyrant who ruled his house with a rod of iron. Beaumont's father did all he could to please him, but it was not to be. It would appear Beaumont has taken up the cudgel and is using it to beat himself. He feels guilty, it's as simple as that.'

Hope considered her mother's words and tried to work out what they meant. 'So the problem is straightforward, is that what you mean, Mama?'

'Yes, I do. Beaumont is a marvellous man. He knows how to bring succour to people and he also knows how to enjoy himself. Remember how easily he took to our bicycling outing and how he was content to let us row? He reminds me of your dear papa in many ways. If only he were here now I'm sure he could counsel Beaumont. Unless . . . '

Hope sprang up. 'What is it, Mama? You have a plan, don't you? Please tell me.'

Prudence smiled. 'We will have to convince him that he is needed.'

'How are we going to do that when he is going away tomorrow?' wailed

Hope. The thought of his departure under such a burden of unhappiness distressed her beyond reason.

* * *

Edna pulled aside the drapes the following morning and Hope sat up in bed. It had been a very long night with little sleep. Today Beaumont was going away. For Edna's sake she tried to be cheerful. The show yesterday had been enjoyed and she didn't want gloom setting in.

'Which dress shall I lay out for you, Hope?' asked Edna, opening the cupboard to reveal the flourishing array of gowns.

Hope didn't care what she dressed in: sackcloth and ashes would have done. But Beaumont was coming to say goodbye and she would dress up for him. 'The ruby red, I think.'

'Are you sure it isn't too dressy for a morning gown?' asked Edna.

'I trust your sense of fashion, Edna,

but I would like to wear it today.'

'Very well. It *is* beautiful.' Edna fussed around with undergarments and soon Hope was transformed into a vision of loveliness.

At breakfast, Hope was surprised to see not only her mother already sitting at the table, but also Aunt Constance. She skirted the table to kiss them. 'How lovely to breakfast with you both,' she said, taking her seat.

'This morning I feel better than I have for a long time. I wanted some company,' announced her aunt. 'While I was confined to my room I heard laughter and conversation from downstairs and I longed to join in. Dear Prudence and Hope, what a difference you have made to the household. It was so quiet and solemn before you arrived. The only other person to treat me without kid gloves after Eustace's death was Beaumont. More and more I see what Eustace must have seen in him. He is a tonic.'

'Then you must tell him, Constance,'

said Prudence, lifting her teacup to her lips. Over the top of it her eyes smiled at Hope.

'I will when I have the opportunity.' Constance cut into her bacon. 'The show yesterday was fun. Is there the possibility of another one soon?'

'Beaumont is going away,' replied Prudence. 'But I shall arrange a concert as you suggested if that is agreeable to you.'

'I am looking forward to it. Especially Stevenson's performance.' Constance grinned and glanced up at Stevenson who looked as if he were almost going to smile.

After breakfast, Hope sat in the morning room chatting to her mother and aunt. She knew Beaumont would call soon and was feeling anxious. Perhaps she should excuse herself and go out into the garden so she could avoid him. Yes, that was the best thing to do. Before leaving the house she picked up one of Uncle Eustace's books, although she was sure she would be unable to concentrate knowing Beaumont was close.

There was a slight chill in the air and Hope was glad of her shawl. Why had she bothered to wear the ruby red dress? But Mama had been very complimentary about it and had thanked Aunt Constance for introducing her to the dressmaker. Mama had such an easy way about her; she was very gracious despite her impetuousness. The birds were singing and the sun was making an appearance now. Her aunt's garden was quite beautiful. Hope sat on a seat under a tree and waited for the time to pass, trying not to think how she would survive without Beaumont's visits to look forward to. She opened the book to look at the illustrations of Pompeii and Herculaneum. A piece of paper fell out and, knowing it was quite the wrong thing to do, Hope smoothed it out. Having finished reading the unsent letter, she tucked it back inside the book, closed her eyes and became lost in thought.

'I find you at last.' The voice shook Hope from her reverie. She turned to see Beaumont very close by. He had a serious look and seemed rather formidable today. 'Both Prudence and Constance know I'm here. In fact it was their idea I came to find you. For some reason they found they had something important to discuss and couldn't accompany me outside.'

Hope knew her mama had plotted the meeting, but the two of them colluding was more than she could understand.

'May I?' Beaumont indicated the grass next to her.

'Please.' As Beaumont settled himself she took a deep breath. 'There is something you must read. But before you do so, I have a question. In what regard did you hold Uncle Eustace?'

'He was a remarkable man. He quietly worked to help people less fortunate than himself. He wanted no reward, not even praise. Your aunt was unaware of many of his good works.

The one regret of his life was that he and Constance remained childless. If I were to mould myself on someone it would be Eustace.'

Hope passed him the note. 'It is a note written by my uncle to you. Whether he ever intended sending it we will never know.'

Beaumont read aloud. 'My dear friend, Mr Beaumont, I am writing with some words of advice. You have many virtues, but you have one major failing. You have taken onto your shoulders the sins of another man, a man you barely knew. You must cast aside the guilt you feel and concentrate on those activities you do best. I know you have worked hard to improve the conditions for your workers in your family mill and have already built bathhouses and alm-shouses. I am confident you will continue with this work as you have a worthy heart. If I had been blessed with a son I hope he would have resembled you. Yours in highest regard, Eustace.'

Hope watched his face as Beaumont

folded the paper and handed it back to her. She was unable to determine his feelings. After an interminable silence he said, 'He is right, as you were yesterday evening. My feeling of unworthiness is a fault I must overcome.' He took a deep breath. 'And now, Hope, tell me your plans.'

Hope didn't want to think of the immediate future when Beaumont would be away, but tried to sound cheerful. 'I expect Mama and I will have some adventures before she returns to Papa and I will continue to teach the maids and anyone else who wants to join the lessons. Although, I did notice that quite a few of the servants were reading the more difficult passages I had written on the pamphlet. Some are reasonably well educated.'

'Indeed they are. I wonder how we could help them.' Beaumont leapt to his feet and reached down to grab her hand and pull her up to face him. 'A lending library at my house. That must be what I set up next. I have heard of it before where benevolent employers provide a lending library for their servants. What do you think, Hope?' He grabbed her and twirled her round in a foolish dance.

'I think it is an excellent idea.'

'My library won't be solely for my own servants, but for the employees of all my friends and acquaintances.'

'Your house will be perfect. In fact . . . '

'Go on.'

'Nothing.'

'Please, I'd like to hear what you have to say,' Beaumont insisted.

'I had a similar thought when I visited your home dressed as Richard. It's the ideal setting from what I could tell.'

'When I saw you looking round I imagined you despairing at its untidiness.'

'No, I liked the atmosphere very much. But it seemed as though the rooms could be put to good use and you have plenty of books.'

'I think the drawing room will make an excellent library. I never use it. Will you help me set it up?'

'I'd like that very much, but haven't you forgotten something? You are going to Yorkshire later today.'

'Aah, now *I* have something to show *you*.' Beaumont pulled a letter from his pocket and waved it under her nose. 'There is no need for you to read it, but the problems my manager was encountering have been solved. It is unnecessary for me to go now although I would like to visit shortly.'

'You could set up a library there for the workers.'

'Another good idea. I believe fate is working to keep us together. The receipt of the letter from my manager was timely. And having postponed my journey I have the opportunity to know you better by spending some time with you, if that will please you. I do not think your mother will disapprove. In fact I have a feeling she might view me as a potential suitor.'

'Shouldn't I have a say in that matter?' asked Hope. It was more than she dared wish for, but she didn't want to appear eager. Also, she was a little vexed that she might not be consulted on the subject. She was aware Mama and Beaumont were capable of anything.

'Of course you should,' replied Beaumont in an even tone. 'Might this convince you?' Hope felt his breath on her face and his features became indistinct as he moved nearer to her. The touch of his lips was gentle yet passionate. She responded to him without a care in the world knowing she wanted to be with him forever. 'My darling Hope. Forgive my forwardness. I know it's contrary to decorum, but when I'm with you I can't help my actions.'

Hope let out a ripple of laughter. 'Dear Beaumont, you don't observe protocol with anyone! You please yourself.' When no reply came, she felt foolish. What had she said to offend him now? His face had grown serious, but he didn't distance himself from her. 'What is it? What have I said that is wrong?'

Beaumont shook his head, his hair brushing Hope's face. 'Nothing at all! You referred to me as 'dear Beaumont'. I am deeply moved and honoured.' His forehead lightly touched hers and it seemed as if a jolt of something powerful leapt between the two of them.

14

The following days passed quickly in a hive of activity. Hope was exhausted by her physical labours. She had taken on the task of sorting Uncle Eustace's books into some semblance of order suitable for the purposes Beaumont and she had in mind. Aunt Constance had been most willing for the books to be put to good use and was taking a lively interest in the process. Some of the time she got in the way and held up the process by chatting about some of the titles. Hope didn't mind; she was delighted her aunt was drawn to the subject. It was good to hear her reminiscences, but it meant the task took a great deal longer than expected. As Hope climbed up and down the library steps to retrieve volumes, Constance took some of them from one pile and placed them onto the other without realising she was doing anything untoward. Prudence understood and at last managed to persuade her sister-in-law to take a turn around the garden.

'The fresh air will do us both good,' she declared, taking Constance's arm. 'Also I want to ask you about your dressmaker. Do you suppose she has the time to make a gown for me? I will need something special for the concert. Most of my clothes are still in Italy.' Prudence steered Constance from the room, turning to raise her eyebrows at her daughter.

'Thank you,' mouthed Hope, smiling broadly. It seemed to her that she had a constant smile on her lips these days. She wiped a hand across her forehead and rearranged the piles of books.

It was a hard job to consider which works would be more suitable for the factory workers and which for the more educated servants. It was easier to discern the needs of the unschooled. The contents of Uncle Eustace's library had nothing suitable for them. Hope decided she would devise her own books. It would give her a great deal of pleasure to do so, but she despaired of having the time and energy to fulfil the undertaking. To her surprise Edna entered the room. She was a welcome sight.

'Have you come to help?' Hope enquired.

'I still have unexpected duties. Mr Stevenson and the cook are taking an inventory of various things to ensure we have enough provisions for the concert.'

'Is it an awful lot of extra work for you all?' asked Hope. She hadn't considered the implications for the staff. Now she was horrified at her lack of thought.

'Oh no, my lady, we are quite excited by it.'

'I am Hope, remember?'

Edna looked about her. 'I wasn't entirely sure you were alone. Outside your rooms I think I should call you by your title.'

There will always be this divide, thought Hope. There would never be a time when people addressed each other by their Christian names with no consideration of what position they held in a household. She noticed something in Edna's hand. 'What have you there? Is it for Mama or Aunt Constance? If so, they are in the garden.'

'No, Mr Stevenson said it's a letter for you.' Edna handed Hope the envelope and hurried off.

Glad of a brief respite, Hope sank into a chair and opened the stiff white envelope. The writing was unfamiliar to her and she couldn't guess who had communicated with her. It took at least two readings for her to comprehend the information in the letter. When she did, it required all her will power to stop herself from screaming aloud and running around the room. Her article about the importance of literacy for the magazine had not only been accepted, but there was a payment as well. She would willingly have forgone the emolument just for the pleasure of seeing her work in print and knowing someone thought it was good enough to be included in a publication. It would be unseemly to return the money, so she would put it towards the lending library.

The contents of the letter gave Hope renewed vitality and she tackled the job in hand with fervour. By the time her mama and aunt returned, she had sorted the piles of volumes she would like to keep. Now she had to find a way to transport them to Beaumont's house; it would be his job to take them to his factory.

'I shall ring for tea,' said her aunt. 'You seem to have disturbed quite a bit of dust from the shelves, Hope. It will be a good opportunity for a thorough clean in here.'

'I don't wish to give the maids more work,' said Hope. That had not been her intention at all. 'I believe they have additional labour because of the concert.'

'Nonsense,' said Constance. 'They always cope admirably.'

Stevenson appeared at the door. 'Excuse me, Your Grace, but you have a visitor. Lady Padstock has arrived with her daughter.'

'We shall come at once,' said Constance. 'Please serve tea in the drawing room.'

After greetings all round the women were soon comfortably seated.

'I have been hearing rumours from my lady's maid that some very strange events have occurred here,' Lady Padstock said, before sipping her tea.

'Strange?' Constance asked. 'Possibly not the word I would have used. My niece and Beaumont have simply opened my eyes to possibilities I would never have thought of. I can say with all honesty that I am happy and that my dear Eustace would be delighted with my new found happiness, the magic lantern show, the reading lessons and the lending library we are setting up together.'

Hope grinned when she heard her aunt include herself so closely.

'Now, my dear,' Constance continued, 'I heard a rumour myself. It is that Isabella rather flouted etiquette at your ball and danced almost every dance with James Henderson.'

Isabella blushed and looked down at the floor.

Lady Padstock puffed out her chest. 'Indeed, it is true. However, I have some news for you. That is the reason for our visit. The Honourable James Henderson has asked for Isabella's hand in marriage.'

Hope smiled at Isabella. 'I am delighted and wish you and James a long and joyful union.'

'I am delighted too.' Constance fiddled with her wedding ring. 'I wish you all the happiness Eustace and I shared, but if you only have half you will be blessed.'

Hope's mama rose and kissed Isabella on the cheek. 'It is wonderful news and I too wish you every happiness.' Seated again, she added, 'It worked then.'

They all turned to her.

'I mean dancing with him for every dance worked. Possibly one should not follow the rules of etiquette. What do you think Hope?'

'Oh, Mama, I don't even know what they are because you have never taught them to me properly. You have let me be unchaperoned with Beaumont, but nothing terrible has occurred.'

'Oh, my dear, is that true?' Lady Padstock looked alarmed.

'Yes, we have become friends. I would happily follow Isabella's example and dance every dance with him.' She had said too much, but she was prepared to shock Lady Padstock even more. 'And I have had my hair cut short. Look.' She tugged the false hair pieces from her own hair. 'It was so that I could dress as a man.' Hope wondered if she'd gone too far with her confession as Lady Padstock looked about to have an attack of the vapours.

As soon as her mother was restored, Isabella stood up and walked round Hope studying her hair. 'It is really very elegant. I believe that one day more women will wear their hair in that fashion. And how easy it will be to care for. Oh, Hope, you can't imagine how happy I am.' She clasped Hope's hand. 'I am so in love with James and I am pleased I was right about Beaumont. I told you after our ball he had grown fond of you.'

'I too could see what was happening. I have always been fond of him in spite of his unorthodox ways, but I did not want you, Hope, to become involved with him because I was not sure how your parents would feel,' sighed Constance. 'Many people find him brusque and difficult. I was responsible for your wellbeing while you were in my house. I didn't want to incur your parents' wrath.'

'I am very happy for him to marry you, Hope.' Her mother smiled at her.

'Has he asked?' Lady Padstock enquired.

'No, no, he has not. Please, let us not speak any more of Beaumont.' Hope felt embarrassed and confused. 'Tell us your wedding plans, Isabella. There must be many things to think of.' Hope was content listening to Lady Padstock and Isabella talk of the preparations for what was to be a grand affair.

Somewhat unsettled by her confessions, Hope turned to her diary.

I am unsure what came over me. Why did I show Lady Padstock my hair and why ever did I admit to dressing as a man and why did I tell her I had been unchaperoned with Beaumont? At least neither Aunt Constance nor Mama chastised me for my honesty. In fact we have had a very pleasant time together and my aunt is in fine form and has been laughing. The only sadness I have felt today is that I have not seen Beaumont. Maybe tomorrow. Or shall I visit him with the books as my excuse?

As soon as Hope heard that her mama was taking Aunt Constance to visit an exhibition the next afternoon, she begged to be allowed the loan of the brougham and a footman to carry the boxes of books.

Beaumont grinned as he ushered her into the drawing room. 'Look! What do you think? I have rearranged it all and there are new shelves to hold the books. And here I have tables for people to sit at.'

'It is quite marvellous, a transformation. I have brought the books from Aunt Constance. Some are for the library here and some are to go to Yorkshire. They are all labelled so you will know what is for where.'

'Thank you and please thank Constance too. Have a seat.' He pulled out one of the upright chairs for her. 'There is something I wish to ask you.'

Hope wasn't prepared to let her feelings soar. Beaumont was too involved in his good works to be thinking of romance. 'Before you ask me your question I have something important to tell you. I have received an acceptance letter and a payment for the writing I sent to the magazine.'

'Congratulations. That is marvellous news and will be an inspiration to all your pupils. You must send off some more work. Now may I ask my question?'

Hope nodded and tried to stay calm.

'When I thought of the idea of a lending library you said you had a similar idea when you first visited my home. I would be interested to know what it was.'

'It seemed a good place to set up a school.'

'We have schools.'

'I suppose I mean a learning establishment for people who are working and want improvement, not for children.'

'Hope, you can't imagine how I wished you to say that. You echo my thoughts perfectly. That's exactly the concept I had. I wasn't sure how I could implement it, but if you are to be my partner then it cannot fail.' His smile bore into Hope's eyes and she felt her lips lift in a besotted smile. To be Beaumont's partner would be simply wonderful.

Pulling herself round, she said, 'Are we to have a school at the expense of a library here? Or can the two work jointly?'

'I think jointly, do you?' Beaumont didn't wait for a reply as he continued, 'The people who come to the library to read books might find themselves drawn to our lessons. We could encompass so many people. It is a dream I should delight in fulfilling. Hope, you have no idea how indebted I am to you.'

'Truly, I have done nothing. Except collect a lot of books.' Together they surveyed the boxes which had been stacked up neatly in the room across the hallway.

'I will organise some tea and then we

must make plans. If you have the time to spare, that is.' Beaumont stood up and then sat down again. 'I'm not usually bewildered, but I confess I feel dazed with all that is happening, or about to happen.'

'It's all right, Beaumont. We'll take it one piece at a time. You attend to tea and I'll start to make notes if you have a pen and some paper.'

'Of course.' Beaumont opened a drawer in a desk which had been pushed against a wall and withdrew paper and a pen. 'Here you are. I won't keep you waiting long.'

When Beaumont returned, Hope had quite an impressive list of things which needed to be done. 'They aren't in any especial order, I simply wrote down my thoughts,' she said, handing him the page. 'Ah, tea, just what I need.' She brought the cup to her lips and sipped at it. 'Oh my goodness!' She hastily returned the cup to its saucer and bit her lip. It would not do to be rude, but the tea was truly unappetising.

'What's the matter? I am not used to preparing tea.' Beaumont peered into the cups. 'It looks a little darker than normal. Did I put in too many leaves?'

'*You* made this?' Hope was astounded. She had imagined the housekeeper to be in the kitchen, but she had seen no sign of any staff at Beaumont's house today.

'Of course. Not very competently apparently.' He took a sip and screwed up his face as he swallowed. 'I think we would do better to follow Prudence's example and have whisky.'

'Well, I don't,' stated Hope, firmly.

Beaumont laughed, sat down beside her and together they discussed the notes Hope had made.

After a while Hope stood up to stretch herself. She had grown quite stiff. Walking to the window, she espied the brougham. The driver's head lolled on his chest as if he was asleep and the footman was walking up and down the pavement — even the poor horse looked weary. How long had she and

Beaumont been ensconced in his drawing room? Too long was surely the answer to that question. She consulted the watch which Aunt Constance had given her permission to wear even though it was a present for her papa. 'I must go,' she said. 'Would you like to keep the list we have made? Or shall I take it and see if I can add to it?'

'Add to it? My goodness, if things are added to its enormous length I can see none of it coming about. We must start simply, Hope. As you said, one piece at a time. Although you've given me a new idea. We could teach people to tell the time. It would be very useful. Not everyone can, you know. Even if one is able to form letters and read words it does not mean they can understand the concept of numbers. Now there's another thing. The possibilities are endless. There is so much we have to organise. So many ideas to develop.' Beaumont was already scribbling things onto the paper and reaching for another sheet.

'When shall we meet again?' she asked him, gasping as she realised her question could be misinterpreted. 'What I mean is, meet to discuss the projects we have in mind.'

'I should be delighted to meet you at any time, Hope. But if we are to progress with our plans, then I'm not sure if I should be near you. You are very distracting to say the least.'

Hope frowned. She couldn't understand how she could be off-putting; she had tried really hard to order her thoughts and be business like. After all, it was an important step they were both taking. Then she realised the implication of his words and felt her heart beating wildly. Was it sensible to be working closely with Beaumont? Her mother wouldn't mind at all, she was sure, but what about Aunt Constance? And what if Lady Padstock found out! Whatever would happen then? All of a sudden she didn't care at all about anyone's opinion except her own and Beaumont's.

15

On the way home, Hope firmly put aside thoughts of being with Beaumont. Instead she considered what he had said concerning her writing. If she could get something else published there would be more money to invest in the school. Reference and workbooks would have to be purchased and although she was sure Papa would endorse her activity and even bestow money towards it, she wanted to be more independent. What could she write? A complete book would take a very long time, she estimated. There were only so many articles she could write as she had little detailed knowledge or learning. Perhaps a slim volume of short stories would be acceptable. But where could she send them? Who would be able to advise her?

At last the brougham carriage arrived

at Aunt Constance's house and she was now in a calmer state to greet her mama and aunt.

'Was the exhibition enjoyable?' asked Hope as she entered the drawing room. The two older women were chatting animatedly and seemed barely aware of her presence. It was good to see them getting on so well together and excellent that Aunt Constance was still in good spirits.

Prudence looked up. 'It was remarkable, darling. You should have come with us. You would have been enthralled.'

Hope smiled as she recalled her own enthralling time with Beaumont. There was so much to think about, to plan, to consider. All she really wanted to do now was to be on her own and recapture their afternoon together. But she must remember her manners. 'I am pleased you enjoyed it. Perhaps I could go another day. Do tell me all about it.'

They showed her pamphlets they had brought from the gallery. The pictures were truly remarkable.

'It would be an achievement to paint like that,' sighed Mama. 'If I could only do half as well . . . '

'I have seen your work, Prudence. You must not underestimate your talent,' Constance admonished. 'There is still a little time before the concert, why don't you paint something for that? Something in keeping with the music to be arranged.'

'A pair of spoons, you mean?' laughed Prudence. Giggles escaped the three of them. 'It is an excellent idea. But I have no easel, no paints. I couldn't do it in the time available.'

'Mama, indeed you could do it. I have paints, you have the ability. What is the theme of the concert to be?'

'After much thought I decided that it should include light music. Something people can relax with. I have selected several songs, some quite witty. Works by Gilbert and Sullivan of course will be included and I have a singer who will surprise us all I feel sure.'

'Oh do tell us who it is,' said

Constance, her eyes alight.

'No, it's to remain a secret,' replied Prudence. 'Hope, I shall accompany you to your rooms and see what paints you have, if you will excuse us, Constance.' Prudence put her arm through her daughter's and led her towards the door. 'Thank you for a lovely afternoon, Constance. I trust I haven't fatigued you too much.'

* * *

When Hope was finally alone in her rooms she dwelt on the events of the afternoon. Her time with Beaumont had been blissful, but now she wanted to concentrate on the days ahead. Several things needed to be accomplished: the library, the school and the concert. Hope knew how her mama behaved when she was painting. She was oblivious to anything else and it would fall to Hope to finalise the details of the concert, she felt certain. Hope would have to ascertain the plans her mother had made. There was still a little time before she need change and go downstairs again, so Hope put everything else out of her mind and started writing a short story which had come to her a couple of days ago.

A knock at her door startled her. Edna entered. 'Hope, Her Grace and Her Ladyship are waiting for you.'

'I was writing and didn't notice how the time has flown by.' Hope put down her pen and stretched her fingers.

'What are you writing?' asked Edna, her eyes darting towards the pages. 'Such a lot of words. Is it a letter? Oh, do forgive me, I don't mean to pry. The talk below stairs is of reading and writing and suchlike. Mr Stevenson and the housekeeper have taken to reading bits from the newspaper to us. When Her Grace has finished with them, of course.'

'This is a story which I would like to be published.'

'What sort of a story is it? A nice romance? Or a gory tale?'

'It's a tale of adventure,' said Hope, 'but you have given me an idea for a further story. I shall dedicate it to you.' She jotted down a few notes so she wouldn't forget her thoughts. 'I must get changed. Mama will be cross with me, although I'm surprised *she's* remembered it's dinner time.'

When Hope entered the drawing room dressed for dinner her mama handed her a parcel with paint-stained hands. 'I forgot to give this to you earlier. It is from your papa.'

Hope ripped off the brown paper to reveal a small box. It was labelled 'You can't please all the people all the time'. 'Here is a letter.' She read it out, 'My dear Hope, since hearing of your fascination with magic lanterns I have been searching for a gift for you. I believe the slides I am sending are quite old, but will please you. If you are able to spare her, please send your dear mama back to me. Your loving Papa.' She held the series of slides up to the light. The story about the ass, the man and his son trying to please everyone made her giggle. Hope longed to rush to Beaumont's house to show him the slides and have the opportunity to see them projected using the magic lantern. It would be disappointing if he already had the same ones.

Stevenson appeared and announced that dinner was served. Hope almost skipped into the dining room and then remembered how selfish she was being. She had completely forgotten to enquire how her mama's painting was coming on.

'Mama, you will believe me to be as observant as Sherlock Holmes, but I deduce you have started on your latest work of art.'

Her mama studied her hands. 'I always was messy. You are right. I haven't had much time, but have started work on the painting for the concert. I am afraid your papa will have to wait for my return to the continent. There are lots of things to do here. I wondered if any of the servants would like to produce some art work. We might have a small exhibition as well as a concert.'

Constance sighed. 'Where will this end? There is one new idea after another.'

★ ★ ★

Although tired, Hope felt too distracted to go straight to bed after retiring to her room. She sat at the escritoire and pulled her journal towards her.

It has been the most marvellous day. There are so many exciting things happening. The concert and exhibition, the library and school and the book I wish to publish. It is little wonder I feel unable to lie down and sleep. And then there is Beaumont. It is quite astounding he attempted to make tea for us. I am sure Papa has never done such a thing. I doubt Papa has even been in a kitchen.

How does Beaumont regard me? Am

I simply a like-minded soul or does he have deeper feelings? The kiss we shared seems to have happened in another life. It was such a long time ago.

Should I visit him tomorrow in order to show him the slides and continue with our work or should I wait for him to call on, or write to, me? I will finish now and go to bed and hope to dream of Beaumont, the man to whom I've lost my heart.

★　★　★

The evening of the concert arrived and again the lively chatter of the servants filled the room, but this time the event was taking place in the drawing room rather than the servants' hall. Before settling themselves on the rows of seats the servants were being encouraged by Prudence to study the exhibition of art work which had been arranged in the dining room.

Hope was seated near the back and

tried to concentrate on the programme in her hand, but couldn't resist constantly turning round to see if Beaumont had arrived. They had seen each other several times in the previous days, but there had been too much to do to have time for anything of an intimate nature to pass between them. He had promised he would be there and she was disappointed when the first item started and there was still no sign of him. Hope knew she should not fidget, but she couldn't help her fingers caressing the beautifully soft silk of her dove grey dress. The purple trimmings were adorable and the gown fitted her well. She had dressed with Beaumont in mind. Now it seemed as if her efforts had been in vain. But, she reminded herself, this concert was not for her to further her acquaintance with Beaumont. With a sigh, she abandoned her selfish thoughts and tried to concentrate on the entertainment.

The audience was appreciative even when the performers were overcome by the grandness of their surroundings and the imposing piano they were expected to play or be accompanied by. One of the footmen had been inveigled into making the announcements.

'And now, Your Grace, Your Ladyships, Ladies and Gentlemen, what you have all been waiting for, Mr Stevenson on the spoons.'

Huge cheers went up as Stevenson stepped forward his face slightly flushed. To his credit, he made a good tune from the instruments. Hope hid a smile as she imagined him practising late at night. Perhaps he concealed himself in a cupboard to muffle the noise. She clenched the insides of her cheeks to prevent laughter escaping. As he came to the end of his piece, applause rang out and Stevenson took two bows. He even managed a full smile and looked quite handsome, Hope thought. She cast a glance towards her mother and aunt, both of whom were looking happy and clapping enthusiastically. The evening was going to be a huge success. But where was Beaumont?

The next performance was a song accompanied by the piano. It was a comic piece and following that was a romantic song delivered with barely-concealed embarrassment and laughter by Edna and one of the footmen. Hope was happy to hear Edna's clear voice ringing out through the drawing room. She clapped loudly at the end of their performance and then her mind was on Beaumont again. Where was he?

She turned towards the hallway, but there was still no sign of him. He wouldn't let her down, would he? Perhaps he'd been taken ill, or had been summoned to his business after all. She waited impatiently for the interval, knowing she should put more effort into the proceedings, but now she was preoccupied and hardly heard the introduction to the next act. The programme twisted in her hands and fell to the floor. As she bent to retrieve it, she heard a melodious voice from the front of the room. Someone was singing and doing it in style. Raising her head, she craned her neck to see who it was. Her intake of breath was audible she was sure. But what a surprise to see and hear Beaumont. His rendition of 'Fair Moon to Thee I Sing' was splendid. Prickles ran up and down Hope's bare arms as she listened. His voice had an overwhelming effect on her, so much so that even after the singing had stopped and the applause died down, she sat in her seat unable to move.

'Hope, Hope, are you all right, darling?' It was Mama. 'It's time for the refreshments. We must circulate, come along. Wasn't Beaumont impressive?'

As if in a dream, Hope followed her mother and oversaw the food and drinks. The servants would feel awkward and shy eating in front of their employers. Hope gave herself a shake and smiled at Molly. 'Take this plate and help yourself,' she encouraged. 'I can recommend the salmon mousse, but remember to leave room for the cakes. They look completely delectable.' She was rewarded with a smile and a thank you from the young girl who proceeded to help herself, inhibitions seemingly forgotten.

'My lady, it's a wonderful evening.' Edna was by her side with a plate full of treats from the refreshment table. 'May I get some food for you?'

'That is most kind, Edna, but I will help myself when everyone else has a plateful. You are here to relax and enjoy yourself.'

'It's a perfect evening. I shall remember it always.' She drifted away with a dreamy look on her face.

'And will you remember it always?' Hope didn't need to turn around to know to whom the voice belonged.

'I shall indeed,' she replied. 'I had no idea you could sing as well.' She faced him and felt her cheeks grow warm.

'As well as what?' Beaumont's eyes twinkled as he gazed down at her.

Hope was lost for words. At last she managed, 'As well as your other talents such as projecting slides and narrating your shows.' Changing the subject would be a helpful option she surmised. 'I think the concert is a success so far. Everyone seems to have entered into it with zeal.'

'And are *you* to entertain us a little later on?' Beaumont enquired. He took a plate from the diminishing pile and helped himself to items from the table.

'No, I shall not, but there is a full programme. Will you stay until the end?' Hope held her breath, wishing with all her might that he would say yes.

'Yes. And there is someone I should like you to meet. A friend of mine. I asked Constance if I could invite him as I needed some moral support before my performance.' He busied himself with the food, forking some of the sliced roasted meats into his mouth.

'I will try to make time for the introduction, but you must appreciate the evening is very full.' Hope started when she felt Beaumont's hand pressed firmly against her back. 'Stop it. We are in a public place,' she hissed.

'I am simply trying to propel you over to my friend. There he is, surrounded by females as usual.'

Hope's good humour waned. She wasn't the sort of woman who was prepared to be pushed around.

'He is a publisher,' Beaumont said.

Her curiosity was aroused. 'What sort of works does he publish?'

'Meet him and ask him yourself.'

Hope and Beaumont spent the rest of the interval with his friend discussing books and publishing. When the bell rang for the second half, Hope was promised that any manuscript she sent in would be given top priority and read immediately.

At the end of the performance Hope had barely stood up before Beaumont joined her. 'Would you care to have a look at the art exhibition with me?' he asked. 'From the comments I have heard there are some very gifted members of staff here.'

'I shall make sure everyone is happy first, but I should like to see the art work.'

When Hope was satisfied she had carried out her duties, they studied the pictures which ranged from pencil drawings to her mother's huge canvas with great coloured swirls depicting roses in their various stages from delicate tight buds to full-blown blooms.

'Roses! The symbol of love.' Beaumont studied the painting. 'Is that how you imagine love, Hope?'

Hope put her head to one side and thought. Love? If she was in love with Beaumont then it was a wonderful swirling feeling, full of colour and light, exactly like the painting. 'I think it might be. What do you think?'

'I have never been in love . . . ' He took Hope's hands in his.

She tried to steady them and hide her disappointment.

' . . . until now,' he added.

'Hope, Hope, have you seen your

mama?' Constance bore down on them.

They dropped hands as though burnt. 'No, Aunt, I have not. Is there a problem?'

'I've had an idea I wish to discuss. We have the Queen's Diamond Jubilee to look forward to and I think I may hold an event of some sort in aid of the Female Aid Society.'

Beaumont became animated. 'That's a marvellous idea, Constance. And you have plenty of time to plan it. I would be happy to help in any way I can. Possibly a magic lantern show with slides of the royal family. I shall see if I can rent some nearer the time.'

'Eustace would be proud of us all.' With that she turned and headed back the way she'd come.

'She is a remarkable woman. But all the women in your family are remarkable as well as beautiful.'

'Dear Mama is beautiful, but I fear I haven't inherited her looks at all. Isabella is exquisite. I wish I looked more like her.' Hope pulled a face and looked at the floor. Why did she have to comment at all? Wasn't she satisfied with being thought of as remarkable? By anyone else certainly, but it was not enough to be regarded thus by Beaumont.

He took her hand and held it tightly. 'Isabella is pretty, but her looks are skin-deep and will fade with the years. Your beauty shines from within and will be ever-present.' He paused briefly. 'Hope I must confess that I knew you were Richard from our very first encounter at the fair. Even from a distance and in the disguise of a man there was never any doubt in my mind that I was in your presence. Your scent, your delicate skin and your eyes, the most beautiful in the whole world, left me in no doubt.'

As far as Hope was concerned at that moment they were the only two people in the universe. Their eyes met and understanding radiated between them. Yes, love was definitely a swirling feeling, full of colour and light. There was no way she could stop her heart pounding or her lips smiling.

In order to relive their time together, Hope wrote down her thoughts when she reached her room.

I believe Beaumont loves me. He said as much. Did he or did I imagine it? What will happen next? What a marvellous evening. Everyone was so happy. Even Beaumont isn't as serious as one might think. He told me that he often puts one of the slides in the lantern the wrong way up so that the audience participate by booing and hissing.

What does my future hold?

I can't wait for tomorrow as Beaumont and I are going to take the works of art from below stairs and hang them at his house in the rooms we are using for the library and school. Then I am to work on some stories for the school. Beaumont's idea is that I copy the pictures from a series of slides onto paper and write captions.

303

In spite of Beaumont's kind words regarding my beauty I need to sleep now so that tomorrow I don't look like a rumpled bedsheet.

★   ★   ★

With the aid of a couple of servants, the paintings and drawings were carefully wrapped and taken in the brougham to Beaumont's house. Prudence insisted on being involved in the process of hanging them thus depriving Hope of any time alone with him. The three of them worked well together and finally they were satisfied with the look of the rooms.

'We must start our lessons soon, Hope. If you are staying in London, Prudence, art lessons would be much appreciated I am sure.'

'It is something I would enjoy, but I will be leaving to join Hope's father in the next few days.'

Now Hope anticipated some time with Beaumont, but it was not to be.

'I have to speak to Beaumont,' said Mama. 'Find a book and read, Hope. I know it's what you enjoy most.'

It used to be. Now she wanted to spend her time with Beaumont. Whatever could they have to discuss that did not include her? Ridiculously, she felt slighted.

'Very well, Mama. Take as long as you like.' She wouldn't let her feelings be known. Her hands trailed along the bookshelves until she came upon a travel book. Reluctantly, she found herself drawn into it from the first page. By the time Mama and Beaumont returned to the room, she was so engrossed, she wasn't aware of them until she heard Beaumont's voice.

'And when will you and your husband return? I would very much like to meet Lord Richmond. As you know there is something of great importance I may wish to ask him.' Beaumont turned and winked at Hope.

Was he teasing? Was he suggesting he would be asking for her hand in marriage? It wasn't possible. How unkind he was to tease her so.

'I think I will make my way back to Constance's house and supervise the packing of my trunks. I know you wish to talk to my daughter in private.'

'Yes, we have much to discuss about the running of the school and the library. Hope has a thousand and one ideas. I have only one.'

It had been difficult to bid Mama farewell; having her close had meant so much to Hope. They'd enjoyed wonderful outings together and many things had been accomplished. Mama made everything seem very easy. You made up your mind what you wanted and then just achieved it. It sounded very simple. If only she could do that and make Beaumont hers. She consoled herself there was a lot to look forward to as the library was scheduled to be opened soon and, after more preparation, the school would take its first pupils. It was a very exciting time.

Also Mama and Papa would be home again in a short while.

★ ★ ★

'Hope, you're looking tired,' said Aunt Constance one afternoon as they were having tea. 'You haven't taken on too much, I trust.'

'No, Aunt, I'm enjoying it. I don't seem to sleep well, though.' She would not divulge the reason for that to Constance. 'I expect I've so many ideas spinning around my head. I should do as Mama does and not worry about things.'

'I think it's something which comes with age,' replied her aunt. 'Things have a way of working out for the best even if we don't always see it at the time.'

'Aunt, thank you for having me to stay with you. I am to be your guest for longer than expected.'

'Hope, you are not a guest. You are family. And may I say that I have come to regard you as a friend. The house

307

will seem very empty when you do leave.'

'You are the kindest, most perfect aunt anyone could have.' Hope rushed to hug Constance who nearly spilt her tea.

'You are very impetuous, child. I don't want my gown ruined.' She put down her cup and brushed at her dress. 'Do you like it?' she asked, sounding shy.

Hope stared. How could she not have noticed? 'You are out of mourning, Aunt. I feel so pleased for you. And you look magnificent in that colour.'

'Eustace liked this dress. And he always said blue suited me. I have you to thank. You and Prudence.'

'Will you visit Beaumont's house and see the library?' Hope wanted to involve her aunt. 'There are lots of Uncle's books there. In fact if it hadn't been for you and him there wouldn't have been a library.' She watched with satisfaction as Aunt Constance's cheeks grew pink and a smile lit her face.

Constance did visit the library and she even borrowed a few books, just to set an example, she explained. The days passed and Hope found herself enjoying the challenges of both the library and now the school. Beaumont and she took turns with lessons and she hardly exchanged a few words with him which were not related to work. He seemed pre-occupied and restless still, but that didn't impinge on his teaching ability.

Then one day he appeared to have a lightness to his step and he laughed and joked with pupils. Hope longed to know what had brought about the change, but felt reticent about asking him. She had noticed an envelope on his desk in a room which was out of bounds to anyone but Beaumont and herself. During a luncheon break, she was allowed into the room and curiosity got the better of her as she peeped at the envelope. It looked extraordinarily similar to her papa's neat lettering. But that would be absurd! Why would Papa be writing to Beaumont? They didn't know each other. It was strange, but she kept the knowledge to herself.

When she arrived home, there was a letter for her also. It was from her mama and papa to say they were returning to England. She checked the date and found they would arrive in London by the end of the week.

Hope was overjoyed. Then she realised she would have to return home with them. What would happen to the library and school she had formed with Beaumont? And what about Beaumont? She would have to leave him. Would Mama let that happen knowing how much he meant to her? The good news had now turned very sour.

★   ★   ★

Edna arrived at Beaumont's house and interrupted a lesson Hope was giving. The maid opened the door to the schoolroom and caught her breath. 'They're here,' she announced.

Hope smiled. Mama and Papa were

at her aunt's house. 'Thank you, Edna. I'll leave as soon as possible.' She turned to her class and explained her situation. Then, after setting them some work to do for the following lesson, she collected her bicycle and rode home.

Sitting between her mother and father, Hope felt extremely happy. Papa held her tightly and kept looking at her. 'I've missed you very much, Hope. It was a most exciting trip.'

'It's lovely to have you back,' replied Hope. 'When will we return to our house?'

'Oh, we're not going back for a few days,' smiled Mama. 'Now I must supervise the unpacking of our clothes. I know your papa will want to visit many places during our short stay in London.'

'You have been up to all sorts of things, I hear,' said Papa. 'Your mama has told me of your escapades. You are so much like her.'

'What else did she tell you?' Hope was anxious to know if her father knew of her attachment to Beaumont.

'Oh, this and that.' Was it Hope's imagination, or was her father being evasive? 'Will you stay and talk with me, Hope? I see you've had your hair guillotined. I think it suits you. Tell me why you decided to do that, then I need to change my clothes as I think Constance is expecting a visitor she wishes me to meet.'

'Oh? Who can that be?' Hope was curious. She had heard nothing of a visitor. Perhaps it was an old acquaintance of Eustace.

'Beaumont!' Hope couldn't stop her cry of surprise. 'What are you doing here?'

'Dear Constance invited me to meet your father,' replied Beaumont. 'It's not an inconvenience to you, I trust.'

'Why don't you two take a walk in the garden? I have a few things to see to,' said her father, shaking hands with Beaumont.

Hope didn't mind walking with Beaumont, but she could detect secrecy and yearned to know what was happening.

No sooner had they reached the holly tree than Beaumont took her elbow and turned her to face him. 'Hope, you must know I care for you deeply. Ever since I first met you I have loved you with a passion. Each time I see you I never want to let you go. Will you be mine for ever?' His eyes never left her as he descended to the ground on one knee. 'Hope Richmond, will you do Mr Beaumont the very great honour of becoming his wife?'

Hope's heart nearly burst out of her dress. 'Mr Beaumont is asking me to marry him?'

'Indeed he is,' replied the gentleman himself. 'And what is your answer?'

'Mr Beaumont, I should feel my life to be complete if I could spend it with you, but only if I may call you Beaumont as that is who I fell in love with.'

Beaumont stood up and crushed

Hope to him. 'My darling,' he whispered, 'I love you with all my heart and soul. At last I feel able to propose marriage to you as I now consider myself to be a worthy man. You have made me understand many things for which I am grateful.'

Hope nestled in Beaumont's arms feeling quite at home there. Then suddenly she pulled away from him. 'What does Father say? I don't pretend to know the etiquette, but I understand you should have asked his permission before proposing marriage to me.'

Beaumont hugged her tightly. 'Hope, I'm afraid your mama and I were a little devious. You remember you were sulking when she came to hang the pictures at my house?'

'I was not sulking . . . ' protested Hope against his coat.

'Shush, that's not important. What *is* important is that your mama conveyed a letter from me to your father asking him for your hand and he replied that he would be delighted if I would take you off his hands.'

'He said *that*?'

'Well, no, not exactly. No, he didn't. Hope you must develop a sense of humour if we are to get on.'

They continued their playful exchanges in between snatching kisses and whispering endearments until the moon rose and stars sparkled in the sky.

'The air is cooling,' murmured Beaumont. 'We must go inside. I would hate you to catch a chill.' As they walked along the garden path, he put his arm lightly around her shoulders. 'What will you find to do after we are married? I hope you won't find married life too dull.'

Hope smiled to herself. How could she ever find life with Beaumont dull? 'I shall have a household to supervise and there will be the library and school to attend to. I trust I shall not have to give up those pursuits. And I should like to continue my writing.'

'Do you have anything in mind to write?'

'I have no doubt I shall think of something.'

'You should write a travelogue,' declared Beaumont.

Hope laughed. 'Whilst the journey from Aunt Constance's to the library at your house is in no way dreary, I do not think I could concoct more than a few lines on a page about it, let alone a complete article.'

'Then I shall have to make plans,' said Beaumont. 'After we are married we shall travel to Paris.'

Hope's imagination ran wild as she thought of the descriptions and pictures in Uncle Eustace's book about Paris she had read not so long ago. To travel to a foreign country in the company of Beaumont was more than she'd dared wish for and the thought of walking by the Seine with her new husband, speaking a few words of French . . . The list inside her head of the things they would do was unending. It made her tremble with excitement. Mama had talked of the Moulin Rouge and the dancing at that establishment. It would be something Hope would enjoy watching. Impulsively, she put her hand up to touch Beaumont's face. 'That would be truly magical.'

We do hope that you have enjoyed reading this large print book.

Did you know that all of our titles are available for purchase?

We publish a wide range of high quality large print books including:
Romances, Mysteries, Classics
General Fiction
Non Fiction and Westerns

Special interest titles available in large print are:
The Little Oxford Dictionary
Music Book, Song Book
Hymn Book, Service Book

Also available from us courtesy of Oxford University Press:
Young Readers' Dictionary
(large print edition)
Young Readers' Thesaurus
(large print edition)

For further information or a free brochure, please contact us at:
Ulverscroft Large Print Books Ltd.,
The Green, Bradgate Road, Anstey,
Leicester, LE7 7FU, England.
Tel: (00 44) **0116 236 4325**
Fax: (00 44) **0116 234 0205**

Other titles in the
Linford Romance Library:

THE DARK MARSHES

Sally Quilford

England, late 1800s: Henrietta Marsh has felt a shadow following her for most of her life. There are whispers among her colleagues that this darkness led to the violent death of her parents. When she is incarcerated in a mental hospital, she charts the events that led her there. Meanwhile, her only friend, and the man she loves, fight to save her. But can Henrietta be trusted, or is she truly mad — and guilty of the heinous crimes of which she is suspected?

BOUND BY A COMMON ENEMY

Lucy Oliver

Tied to the violent Edmund by a betrothal contract, Elizabeth Farrell gains an unexpected opportunity for deliverance when their bridal party is stopped in the forest by a band of men. William Downes offers to pay off her contract — if she will enter a temporary marriage of convenience with him instead. Scarred by his past, William refuses to consider marrying for love, but needs a bride to protect both his sister's illegitimate child and the family's land. Will Elizabeth accept the bargain?

TIME FOR CHANGE

Chrissie Loveday

1977: William Cobridge has sold the factory and taken early retirement, but his wife Paula can't help but feel that something is still missing from her life. She wants to move to a smaller, more modern house, but knows that Nellie, her mother-in-law, will never accept the change. In fact, Nellie isn't really coping with anything at the moment . . . Meanwhile, William and Paula's daughter Sophie is sharing a flat with her Aunt Bella, who is exasperating both as her flatmate and boss at work — and Sophie wants out . . .

A SMOKY MOUNTAIN CHRISTMAS

Angela Britnell

Gill Robinson's fiancé has called off their Christmas Eve wedding, and she's dreading the upcoming holidays. Out of the blue, she has the chance to escape: her Aunt Betsy has a small B&B in the Smoky Mountains and needs a break, so Gill flies out to help. But when she meets handsome, enigmatic Luke Sawyer, she knows the quiet time she'd envisioned isn't going to happen. Ostensibly the inn's handyman, Gill suspects there's a lot more to Luke than he's letting on . . .